MW01518659

Book Four of *The Methuselah Chronicles*

Crista's Story

A Novel

by

Terry Lee Hamilton

Foreword by
Pastor John Jones

*Dedicated to Joy and Casey King,
my fantastic daughter and
favorite son-in-law.*

All scripture quotations are from the
King James Version of the Bible.

© 2004

First Edition

Library of Congress
Control Number: 2004114012
ISBN 0-9660753-3-1

Published by
Glory to Glory Ministries
1813 E. 45th St.
Ashtabula, OH 44004
e-mail: terry@glorytogloryministries.com
www.glorytogloryministries.com

Table of Contents

Table of Contents continued . . .

Foreword

I, having just finished reading *Crista's Story*, the fourth novel of *The Methuselah Chronicles*, have several things that come to mind. My first thought is that "finally I know what happened to Crista!" If you have read the previous novels in this series, you know that we have waited a long time to have this part of the story revealed. It was Dr. John Morris, President of the Institute of Creation Research, who said in a previous Foreword in this series: ". . . All of us are waiting for the succeeding volumes. We want to know -- What happened to Crista?"

My second thought is about the author of this series, Terry Lee Hamilton. What an imagination! He has given to us Biblical truth that he has wrapped up in fictional but quite plausible history and has done so in an interesting, exciting, and thought provoking way. This book is both informative and enjoyable (which is quite rare today), and draws you into its sometimes sad, sometimes mysterious, sometimes quite humorous story line and leaves you wanting more.

Lastly, as I read this book, my thoughts turned again to the scriptures and the "progression" or "regression" of mankind into ungodliness and rebellion against God that precipitated the great flood of Noah's day. Wicked humanistic philosophies and practices became more prevalent; although those believers who loved God and looked for the Redeemer struggled in this environment, their faith and their fortitude was still noticed and blessed by our Lord.

While the Biblical account of these people is certainly accurate, our knowledge of their day-to-day lives, experiences, and struggles is quite limited. *Crista's Story* and the entire *Methuselah Chronicles* is a well researched and thoughtful account that, although fictional, allows us to better understand this fascinating period of history and the struggle of the godly in the midst of an ever increasingly ungodly world. It is indeed a message of hope.

Pastor John Jones

Preface

I can truly say that writing *Crista's Story* was a labor of love. Before I began to write Book Four of *The Methuselah Chronicles*, I already had a general outline of what would happen to Crista, but I did not know exactly how the story would flesh out. I was very pleased with how the story turned out.

Before you begin reading this story, please allow me a minute to explain four aspects of my storytelling. First of all, as I began to write this book, I desperately missed the characters of Enoch and Arphaxad, who were translated to Heaven at the end of Book Three, *Bound for Glory*. Those two characters had such a warm, humorous relationship, I felt that the book series could never replicate that depth of character and humor. I am pleased to report that my initial feeling was wrong.

Second, *The Methuselah Chronicles* has always had action, adventure, and humor, as well as character study and sound exposition of this initial Biblical era. But *Crista's Story* adds a new dimension -- it is also a very special love story. I hope you like this new element.

Third, *Crista's Story* does not end where I originally intended it to end. But as I was writing this book, Crista's adventures were so bountiful, I came to realize that Book Four, *Crista's Story*, would have to deal with the last 240 years of Crista's life, while Book Five, *The Road to Noah*, would tell the next 116 years of Crista's story.

Finally, let me say that I love the ending of this book; but I do realize that it is truly a cliffhanger. Have no fear! Book Five has already been written and will be published within a few months after Book Four is published. Enjoy! To God be the glory!

Cast of Characters

(in alphabetical order)

Abel, the second son of Adam and Eve

Adah, daughter of Elam and Bildah; former priestess of the cult of the Great Ebony Cow; wife of Arphaxad

Adam, the first man; husband of Eve; father of Cain and Abel

Aram, younger brother of Enoch; a priest of the cult of the Great Ebony Cow

Arphaxad, Zaava's half brother; ex-thug who became Enoch's traveling companion; husband of Adah

Bildah, wife of Elam; mother of Elihu and Adah

Cain, first son of Adam and Eve; founder of the City of Cain and the cult of the Great Ebony Cow

Captain Blackheart the elder, a slave trader; captain of the *Lucky Lady*

Captain Blackheart the younger, also a slave trader and captain of the *Lucky Lady*

Crista, daughter of Enoch and Sarah; sister of Methuselah

Elam, neighboring farmer and friend of Enoch; husband of Bildah; father of Elihu and Adah

Elihu, son of Elam and Bildah; best friend of Methuselah

Enoch, shepherd and prophet; son of Jared and Rachel; husband of Sarah; father of Methuselah and Crista

Eve, the first woman; wife of Adam; mother of Cain and Abel

Jabal, eldest son of Lamech-Cain; developer of animal husbandry in the City of Cain

Jared, husband of Rachel; father of Enoch

Jubal, middle son of Lamech-Cain; founder of the School of Music in the City of Cain

Lamech, eldest son of Methuselah and Martha; marketing director of Tubal Enterprises

Lamech-Cain, founder of the School of Humanism in the City of Cain

Leah, wife of Captain Peleg

Letch, first mate on the *Lucky Lady*

Lilith, a high priestess of the cult of the Great Ebony Cow

Ludim, a blacksmith in the City of Gom; husband of Perna; father of Tubal; adoptive father of Martha

Martha, a slave girl rescued by Enoch; wife of Methuselah; mother of Lamech

Meshach, husband of Opal; father of Sarah

Methuselah, shepherd; son of Enoch and Sarah; brother of Crista; husband of Martha; father of Lamech

Og, a thug formerly employed by Tubal and Zaava

Opal, wife of Meshach; mother of Sarah

Peleg, a crusty old captain and slave trader who was saved through Enoch's preaching; husband of Leah

Perna, wife of Ludim; mother of Tubal; adoptive mother of Martha

Rachel, wife of Jared; mother of Enoch

Sarah, daughter of Meshach and Opal; wife of Enoch; mother of Methuselah and Crista

Theron, chief priest of the cult of the Great Ebony Cow

Tubal, son of Ludim and Perna; husband of Zaava; founder of Tubal Enterprises

Tubal-cain, youngest son of Lamech-Cain; developer of the metals industry in the City of Cain

Zaava, a high priestess of the cult of the Great Ebony Cow; wife of Tubal

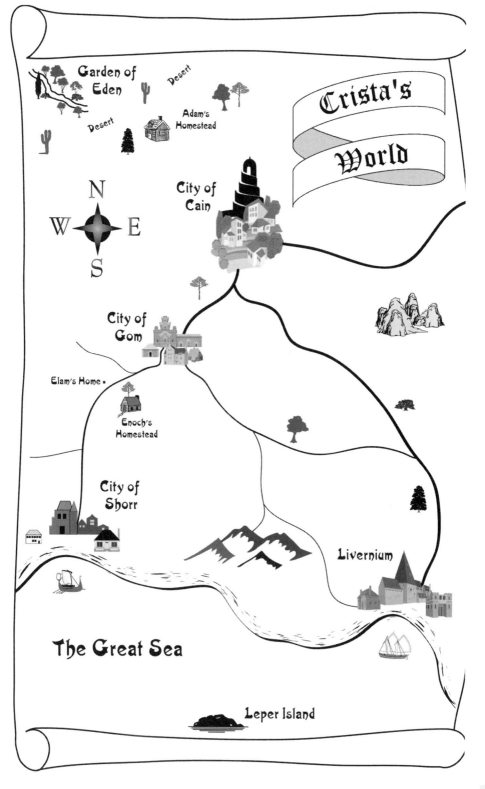

Prologue

1653 A.C.

As he approached the door, the man with the flowing, white beard listened intently for any sounds coming from the room ahead. Can't hear a thing, he said to himself, wondering if his hearing was failing. After all, he thought, I am nearly six hundred years old, and I've been putting up with the pounding of hammers for over one hundred years.

He stopped just outside the door, pausing to listen again for any familiar noises. The first sounds that he heard were sounds from outside the house -- the cawing of crows, the pounding of hammers. No wonder the ancient one often complains about the hammering all day long. I can't hear myself think.

As he blocked out the exterior noise, the listener finally heard something emanating from inside the room, the low but familiar sound of rhythmic breathing. He quickly peeked around the corner and spotted the ancient one with his head on his oaken desk, sound asleep and snoring. Grandpa hasn't had much energy since his heart attack over a year ago.

The man tiptoed into the room, hoping not to disturb the sleeper, hoping that none of the old hardwood floor planks in Enoch's homestead would announce his entrance. Slowly, he walked toward the desk, wondering how much progress the ancient one had made that morning in starting the next volume of *The Methuselah Chronicles*.

As the man neared the desk, he craned his neck forward to see how much had been written. The page was blank.

Just then, the ancient one opened his eyes. "Noah!" he started, "how dare you disturb your grandfather's writing!"

Noah just smiled down on the ancient one. "Grandpa, you seem to be getting more napping done than writing."

"Napping!?! Preposterous!" bellowed Methuselah. "I was just engaged in deep prayer and contemplation about the outline and title of the book."

"Is my name in the title?" Noah teased. "You promised me that you would finally start writing about me."

"Fret not, young man," he counseled. "I'll be getting around to you sooner or later. But remember," Methuselah cautioned, "the thrust of this book is about your great aunt, not you!"

"Well," Noah asked, "have you come up with a title yet?"

"I'm not sure yet. The Lord has given me several ideas, but I haven't settled on one yet."

"How's this for a title?" Noah joked: "Noah's Great Aunt."

"I am not amused, young man," Methuselah responded gruffly. "Be patient. Your time will come. But this next book is Crista's story, not Noah's."

"That's it!" Noah interjected.

"That's what?" Methuselah replied.

"The title of your book -- *Crista's Story*."

"Hmmm," the ancient one mused.   *"Crista's Story*? Not a bad title. I'm glad I came up with it." Then he turned to his grandson and complained: "Now please, leave me in peace. You are disturbing my concentration." Methuselah grabbed his quill, dipped it in the ink bowl, and began to write.

Part One

Crista's Homecoming

940 A.C.

Chapter One

A Trap?

He suspected a trap.

The path was quiet, too quiet, just like before.

The last time he was on this path, he was with his father and Arphaxad; this time, he was alone.

The last time they were on this path, they were being stealthily watched by Cain's priestly assassins. This time, Methuselah was more careful. He left the path and made his way through the trees toward Adam's homestead. This time, the way would be longer, but safer.

Every hundred yards, he stopped and listened for voices. Like the last time, he didn't hear any.

*   *   *   *

As he neared Adam's homestead, Methuselah's mind raced as he recalled the events of the last few days. The miracle of finding his leprous sister Crista at Adam's homestead was immediately followed by the greater miracle of her healing in the wilderness. But their joy was short lived when they were captured by Cain and Zaava, then taken to the Tower of Cain to be executed. Cain and Zaava's murderous plan was perfect, except for one flaw: they were fighting God, not man.

Methuselah would never forget the hopeless feeling as he reeled on his hands and knees atop the Tower of Cain, bent over with merciless spasms of nausea. He would never forget his helpless agony as Zaava's spear sped toward Enoch's heart, only to be intercepted by Arphaxad in a selfless, sacrificial act of love. He would never forget a berserk Zaava, in a last desperate attempt to shove Enoch off of the Tower, stumbling off the Tower platform herself, falling, falling, falling into the flaming pit below.

Methuselah would never forget the sight of his father picking up the dying Arphaxad, then both of them being enveloped in a misty, funnel-shaped cloud, lifting them into the air above the Tower. He would never forget the deep, rolling voice of God filling the sky, proclaiming "I am the Resurrection and the Life." He would never forget the lifeless body of Arphaxad standing erect, taking the spear out of his own body, holding it high over head, then dropping it harmlessly to the platform below.

Methuselah would never forget the dread that encompassed him when Cain reached down to pick up the spear, then flung it straight at Enoch's heart. But the dread turned to amazement as the spear never pierced the cloud, but rather raced around and around the swirling mist, around and around and around until the spear hurtled back toward a stunned Cain.

Methuselah would never forget the moment when the spear struck Cain in the chest. Reeling from the impact, Cain dropped the staff of God. Methuselah remembered how desperately he crawled toward the fallen staff of God, reaching it and grabbing it in an attempt to regain his footing. Methuselah remembered looking up and seeing Cain grab the other end of the staff, tugging to regain its control. Methuselah would never forget the mortally wounded Cain losing the brief tug of war, then stumbling backward, teetering on the edge of the platform, then toppling over into the flaming pit below.

The events on the Tower platform were a life changing experience for Methuselah. Not only did he see the power of God over nature and death, but he also saw the power and grace of God using the unlikeliest person -- a nauseous, helpless coward -- to retrieve and be the bearer of the staff of the tree of life.

And now, as he neared the end of his journey to Adam's homestead to rescue his sister Crista, Methuselah's mind raced back hundreds of years earlier, when he had failed to rescue his sister on that infamous day when she was kidnapped. "I may have failed Crista before," he said with newfound determination, "but I will not fail my sister again!"

*   *   *   *

As he neared Adam's homestead, Methuselah could still hear no voices. It must be a trap.

He crawled on his hands and knees through the trees on the hill overlooking Adam's home. As he reached the top of the hill and peered over, he was nearly blinded. The white, blinding sand of the desolate wilderness had completely surrounded Adam's home, except for one spot near the lonely tamarisk tree. "Adam must be dead," Methuselah whispered sadly to himself.

Methuselah consciously willed his breathing to stop so he could listen for voices. He could still hear none. He could see no one in the woods, around the house, or in the yard. They may be hiding in the house or behind the sand dune.

The sun was descending behind the sand dune. I'll wait until dark, then sneak up on the house, he thought to himself. I must find out what happened to Crista.

Methuselah was reluctant to go down below, scared of what he might find, but even more frightened to go through life without trying to find out what happened to his sister. "After all these hundreds of years, Lord," he prayed, "to finally find her and then to lose her again. It's just not fair, Lord. It's just not fair."

Summoning every ounce of courage, Methuselah started to crawl down the hill, taking cover behind every tree and bush, getting as close to the house as possible without breaking into the open. Crouching behind the bush closest to the house, he took several deep breaths to control his fear, then listened intently for voices or other noises. Nothing! They must be waiting inside, he thought to himself.

He had to know. Taking the staff, he crawled through the sand, as silently as possible, aiming toward the front porch, expecting a priestly guard to burst through the door any moment and pierce him through with a spear.

When he reached the east side of the porch, he flopped down in the sand, breathing hard, more from fear than from fatigue. Putting his ear to the side of the house, he listened again for voices. Nothing. The place is as quiet as a tomb, Methuselah thought. Maybe Adam and Crista are both already dead. But Methuselah was resolved. I must find out. I will not abandon my sister again.

A wave of nausea started to swell within him. Breathing deeply, Methuselah repeated quietly, "I will not abandon my sister. I will not abandon my sister." When the spasm of sickness passed, he rose to one knee, trembling but prepared to step onto the porch.

Just then, the wind whistled through the trees, causing Methuselah to fall face first on the sand in a panic. Looking up, he expected to see a whole squad of assassins swooping down the hill, spears flying toward his exposed body. To his amazement, there was nothing but trees swaying in the night.

Methuselah took several more deep breaths and once again prepared to step on the porch. Suddenly, a new threat appeared from the other direction. A fierce west wind began to howl, blowing sand toward the house, toward Methuselah. His only thought was of the sand dune marching toward the house, swallowing him up along with whoever else was inside. I must find out what happened to Crista, before it's too late.

Leaning on the staff, Methuselah rose to one knee, then gingerly placed his right foot on the porch. Maybe the howling wind will mask any creaking of the boards. He softly tiptoed the few feet to the front door, then stood beside it, facing westward. At the same moment, the wind whipped sand into Methuselah's face, causing pain he had never felt before. I can't stay out here, he cried to himself. But I don't know what's on the other side of the door. He grabbed the door handle, prayed "Lord, save me," then opened the door.

No one came rushing through the door. The only rushing came from the wind and sand blowing into Adam's common room. Turning his back to the sand and taking a deep gulp of air, Methuselah stepped through the door.

He could see nothing. He ducked down, closed the door softly, then took more deep breaths. When his heart stopped pounding, he listened for sounds from inside the house. Nothing.

He stayed low, feeling his way through the common room. Nothing, nobody was stirring. Maybe they are in the courtyard. As he approached the courtyard, Methuselah got down on his hands and knees, groping his way along the furniture and walls, hoping and praying that he wouldn't grope somebody's leg.

A dim shadowy light shone in the courtyard, open to the moon and stars. As his eyes fully adjusted to the light, Methuselah could make out the oven, the water pots, and the cooking table. Something on the table looked like a loaf of bread. Someone has been here recently, he realized, sending a new wave of fear over his body. As he slowly raised to his feet and wandered through the courtyard, all he could think was, Where is Crista? Where is my sister?

At last, he reached the door to the suite of bedrooms in the back of the house. Were the priestly assassins waiting for him on the other side of the door? Were Adam and Crista already dead, lying in a pool of blood on their beds? I must find out.

Methuselah put his ear to the door. Nothing. He stood to the side, slowly opened the door, and waited for something, or someone, to rush through. Nothing. Will I ever find out what happened to my sister?

Methuselah softly stole into the hallway, leaving the door open for a minimum of light from the courtyard. Nothing was in the hallway. No one was there. "Maybe they are in one of the bedrooms. Lord, help me to find them." He didn't know which bedroom was Crista's, but he remembered clearly that Adam's bedroom was the first one on the right.

Methuselah tiptoed to the door, barely breathing, listening for voices inside. Nothing. Just as he was about to tiptoe to the next bedroom, Methuselah heard a voice.

Chapter Two

Bound for Glory

For hours, Crista had been sitting in a chair at Adam's bedside, holding his shriveled, leprous right hand in her hands of baby smooth skin, listening to his breathing become shallower and shallower. The only time that she got up was to light the candle as the sun went down. The sun is going down on Adam's life, she cried. Is it going down on mine also?

Adam's hand was slowly losing its warmth. It won't be long now. During the last two hundred years, she had nursed many people through their dying moments. At least Adam was dying peacefully, unlike so many others. As Crista looked out the window at the stars shining in the moonless night, she thought of Heaven, where Adam would soon join his beloved wife Eve.

As she held Adam's hand and listened to his breathing, the ancient one moved restlessly, opened his eyes, and whispered: "I see her." His lips curled into a smile as he said, "Eve, I'm coming home."

Crista felt a tiny pressure on her hand as Adam prepared for his final journey. Then he whispered, "I see Abel. I see my son." A deep sigh flowed from Adam's throat as the long wait of over nine hundred years to see his beloved son again was almost over.

Then Adam's eyes blinked as he expressed the unexpected. "I see . . . Enoch . . . and Arphaxad." A dart of pain stabbed Crista's heart as Adam's eyes lowered to hers, seeing the tears starting to roll down her cheeks like glowing embers in the candlelight. He sighed again, and speaking directly to his caretaker, he softly uttered, "I'm so sorry, Crista." As she turned her eyes away, she heard Adam softly gasp. "I see . . . Methuselah?"

Crista's heart sank. "Not Pumpkinhead!" she cried.

* * * *

As the door to Adam's bedroom creaked fully open, Crista turned quickly to face the new threat. "Yep! It's Pumpkinhead." She dropped Adam's hand, flew out of her seat, and rushed to the door to embrace her brother. Tears flowed like a river, her body heaving with sobs, overjoyed with his safe return. As he stroked her hair and held her tight, Methuselah watched as his sister slowly controlled her sobs, then wondered with a girlish voice: "Pumpkinhead, I thought you were dead."

"I survived, Crista." Then he held out his walking stick and proclaimed, "As did the staff of God."

She leaned back, stared at the staff of God which her father had used to heal her of leprosy just days before, then focused her gaze into her brother's brown eyes and asked the dreaded question: "And Dad?"

"I'm afraid he's gone, Crista."

As Crista nestled her head into her brother's shoulder again, Adam whispered brokenly, "Methuselah, I . . . saw . . . your father . . . in Heaven."

Methuselah smiled down on the old man. "Yes, I know. I saw him go."

Crista moved back again from her brother's arms. "You, you were with him at the end?"

"Yes," he calmly replied.

Crista bit her lip, then asked another difficult question. "How did he die?"

*   *   *   *

Methuselah smiled. "He didn't."

Crista looked blankly at her brother, then countered, "But Adam just saw Daddy in Heaven."

Methuselah replied, "Zaava and Cain tried their best to kill Father, but they failed." He then explained to the dumbfounded faces of Adam and Crista how Arphaxad died, how Enoch lifted him up, how the swirling, misty cloud came down from Heaven to lift them up, how Arphaxad was raised to newness of life, and how the cloud whisked the two men to Heaven.

"Glory be!" Crista exclaimed.

"Unheard of," Adam weakly uttered. "Death lost her prey." Then a stab of pain entered his heart. Gasping, he asked, "And . . . my son . . . Cain?"

Methuselah looked down sadly, grasped Adam's shriveled hand, and shook his head, briefly describing how the spear struck Cain in the chest and how Methuselah won the brief tug of war for the staff of God. A tear crawled down the ancient one's withered cheek as he slowly uttered, "I shall not . . . see him . . . where I am . . . going."

Adam closed his eyes for the final time, then gave his final blessing upon Methuselah. "Son," he rasped, "the staff of God . . . has fallen . . . to you." With an effort, the ancient one exhorted, "You must . . . pick it up."

*   *   *   *

With a gasp, Adam whispered, "Please . . . both of you . . . hold my hands . . . and sing me a song."

Methuselah was unsure, but Crista directed him to sit on the other side of the bed from her. Holding his hands, the two began to softly sing:

> They that wait upon the Lord
> shall renew their strength.

Unheard by Crista and Methuselah, the duet became a quartet as angelic voices joined in the song.

> They shall mount up with wings as eagles;
> they shall run, and not be weary;
> and they shall walk, and not faint.
> They that wait upon the Lord
> shall renew their strength.

While the two youngsters sang, a smile crossed Adam's lips. "I hear them," he softly uttered. With his eyes closed, he listened to the angelic voices, then whispered, "I see them." Methuselah was confused. "Who?"

Adam opened his mouth slightly. "My friends are coming for me."

"Who?" Crista repeated.

"My cherubim friends from the Garden of Eden. Don't you see them?"

Brother and sister looked heavenward, but could not see what Adam saw. As they turned back, Adam loosened his grip on their hands and extended his arms upward.

Tears began to fall again from Crista's eyes as she whispered, "Say hello to Father . . . and Lilith."

And tears began to fall from Methuselah's eyes as he choked, "Say hello to Martha . . . and the children."

* * * *

Unseen by human eyes, the cherubim hovered over Adam's bed as Adam softly uttered his last words: "Welcome, my friends! I have missed you."

The cherubim spoke in unison. "We have missed you, too, my friend." Then they reached their arms toward the ancient one and said, "We have been given the honor of escorting our old friend into the presence of the Lord." As they grasped Adam's celestial hands and lifted him into the air, the limp arms of the earthly Adam fell to the bed.

Chapter Three

Saaga

Methuselah and Crista buried Adam's old body under the lonely tamarisk tree during a lull in the sandstorm. Then they grabbed a few of Crista's belongings and slogged through the renewed sandstorm up the hill overlooking Adam's homestead. The hill was already covered in the advancing sand. When they reached the top of the hill, they glanced back toward Adam's homestead and the lonely tamarisk tree, which were already being obliterated from man's view.

Crista paused, reminiscing about the loss of her good friend and the loss of her home for the last three years. As the stinging sand burned her face, Methuselah yelled into the wind, "Let's go home, Crista. Let's go home."

*   *   *   *

Methuselah was grateful to leave the sandstorm behind. As they reached the wooded path leading south-easterly, Crista remarked to her brother, "I've watched the desert wilderness advance toward Adam's homestead for three years, Methuselah. I never thought I would live to see the day that Adam and his homestead would be gone."

Methuselah's mind raced back to less than a year ago when he left his homestead behind. Seeing a dark cloud cross over her brother's face, Crista wondered aloud what was on his mind. He told his sister that there was a lot of family news to catch up on. When Crista remarked that she knew quite a bit of the family history, Methuselah asked if she knew he had been married. When Crista cheerily mentioned Martha's name, an even darker cloud passed over Methuselah's face. Crista gasped, stopped dead in her tracks, and asked, "Don't tell me something is wrong with Martha and your children?"

Methuselah turned to look at his sister. "Martha and most of my children were brutally murdered by the giant thug Og last year."

Crista gasped again and stared at her brother as tears started pouring out of his eyes. She grabbed her brother and held him, and they cried together on the path for a long, long time. As her brother sobbed in her arms, Crista's mind replayed the scene just a few days earlier when she had been healed of leprosy, and then they discovered that Cain had set a trap. Recalling the scene back at Adam's homestead of the circle of priestly assassins, with Cain and Zaava in the middle standing next to a giant thug holding a knife to Adam's throat, Crista realized that the giant thug must have been Og. No wonder, she thought, that my brother went berserk. He wasn't trying to protect Adam. He was trying to avenge the murder of his wife and children.

*   *   *   *

Slowly, Methuselah stopped crying and told the story of how his homestead, land, and sheep had been poisoned over a long period of years by agents of Zaava and Cain, and how his oldest son Lamech left the hard scrabble life on the farm to work with Zaava's husband Tubal in the city, and how Zaava assigned Tubal's manservant Og to destroy Methuselah's family. "It's been almost a year, sis," he sniffled, "and I still haven't gotten over it."

Crista patted her brother on the back, said how sorry she was, and then added knowingly, "There will always be a huge hole in your heart, brother." As they continued walking, Crista added, "And I'm sorry I never got to meet Martha and the children."

Methuselah was quiet for a long time as they walked down the path. Eventually, he looked over at his lovely sister, with baby smooth skin and a glow upon her face, such a stark contrast from the hideous Leper Lady of just a few days ago. And then he thought of his lovely Martha, brutally murdered, her body burned virtually beyond recognition. One day, he thought, I'll see her again, and she'll have baby smooth skin and a glow upon her face, too.

Finally, he turned his face toward Crista again and suggested, "Enough of my troubles, sis. Why don't you fill me in on what you have been up to for the last two hundred and forty years." And she did.

*   *   *   *

Of course, the only way home led through the City of Cain. As they neared the city, Methuselah pointed out the Tower of Cain. "That tower was the launching pad where Father and Arphaxad left on their final journey to Heaven."

"I wish I could have been there, Pumpkinhead. I am so proud of you for defeating the wicked Cain."

Methuselah was flabbergasted. "What!?! All I did was puke my guts out, using the staff of God to try to get to my feet. Cain really killed himself."

His sister smiled. "That's your version. I wonder what the people of the City of Cain think."

"Well, sis, I guess we are about to find out."

* * * *

As Methuselah and Crista entered the north gate, a buzz swept through the crowd and people started pointing at the couple. The further they walked up the center street toward the marketplace and temple, the greater the buzz from the crowd, which seemed to divide in front of them. "What are they saying, Crista?" her brother asked.

"They keep crying out your name, brother."

"Yes, but what else are they saying?"

Crista wondered. "It sounds like the people are crying out, 'It's Methuselah the Mighty Cain Killer!'"

Methuselah closed his eyes for a moment, astonished at the crowd's reaction, thinking that they would tear him limb from limb for killing their beloved ruler. His heart pounded, wondering what it would feel like to have his arms ripped from his body.

As they neared the marketplace, there was a commotion up ahead. The multitude scattered as a squadron of guards, spears held high, approached Methuselah and Crista. Methuselah stopped dead in his tracks, wondering where he could hide, how he could escape the inevitable capture and torture. His sister gripped his hand tightly and murmured, "Be brave, my brother."

As the guards neared their prey, they did something entirely unexpected. In unison, they knelt on their right knee and loudly proclaimed, "Hail, Methuselah the Mighty Cain Killer." Then, the entire throng knelt likewise and repeated, "Hail, Methuselah the Mighty Cain Killer." Methuselah looked over at his sister in bewilderment, shrugging his shoulders, and whispering, "I never expected a reception like this."

The guards rose to their feet and surrounded the prized couple, shoving other people aside, as they marched Methuselah and Crista to Cain's mansion. Methuselah marveled at its enormous size. Combined with the priestess house next door, the two buildings filled an entire city block.

As he climbed the steps to the front door of Cain's mansion, Methuselah recalled the stories that he had heard about the giant common room, the twenty chandeliers, the thirty-foot high ebony cow, and the golden throne upon which Cain sat. I wonder, he thought, who is sitting on the throne now?

As the guards led them into the room, the first thing that Methuselah noticed was that the gargantuan ebony cow was gone. Then he spotted a man, much younger than Cain, sitting on the throne. Methuselah had never seen him before. He had long, curly blonde hair, bronze skin, and was holding a book in his hand.

He was wearing a simple white toga, not a royal robe. Methuselah's first impression was that this new ruler was a simple, unpretentious man. The people surrounding the throne were likewise dressed in simple, white togas.

Crista leaned toward her brother and asked, "Do you know who that man is?" When Methuselah shrugged, Crista whispered his name: "Lamech-Cain. Be careful. He's a snake."

Methuselah was confused. How in the world could his sister Crista know that the man sitting on the throne of the City of Cain was Lamech-Cain? And how could she have formed such an ill opinion of such a well favored, powerful man?

As the contingent stopped before the throne, Lamech-Cain looked up. "Ahh," he said gently and with some awe, "if it's not Methuselah the Mighty Cain Killer."

Methuselah did not know how to respond. He just slightly bowed his head as Lamech-Cain ordered the guards to leave, leaving only Methuselah, Crista, Lamech-Cain, and his advisors in the great common room.

"I am so honored to meet you, Methuselah," Lamech-Cain softly spoke. "Please introduce me to your beautiful acquaintance."

Methuselah's only thought was to answer, "This is my sister Crista." Crista did not slightly bow her head.

"Ahh, the children of the recently departed Enoch," replied Lamech-Cain. "Allow me to introduce my children." In turn, Lamech-Cain proudly introduced his sons Jabal, Jubal, and Tubal-cain, each of whom smiled and gently bowed. "I am certain that Enoch was just as proud of his children as I am of mine."

Methuselah, mesmerized by Lamech-Cain's apparent gentleness and love of family, was startled when his sister spoke up: "I should like to also meet your wives and daughter."

Lamech-Cain blinked. Then he blinked again. Methuselah struggled with conflicting thoughts during the pause in conversation. Was his sister's comment rude, or just curious? Were there more members of Lamech-Cain's family than the handsome sons standing near their father? And what did Crista mean by the word "wives"? Wives? That didn't make any sense. God gave one wife to Adam, not two.

Lamech-Cain finally spoke. "Of course, Crista, you would be interested in the female side of the family. Perhaps you can meet them someday." Turning to Methuselah, he quickly changed the subject. "Methuselah, I want to personally thank you for all that you did at the Tower of Cain the other day."

Methuselah was almost speechless. What's he thanking me for? he thought. "I didn't do anything," he mumbled in reply.

"Ah, Methuselah," Lamech-Cain beamed, "you are too humble. By killing Cain, you are personally responsible for ridding the world of his stupid cow religion."

Methuselah mumbled again, "I did?"

"Yes," Lamech-Cain continued, "and at great personal sacrifice. I am so sorry for you and Crista for the loss of your father. I also lament his untimely death as another useless fatality in the insane conflict between competing religions."

Methuselah was completely befuddled by Lamech-Cain's words. He muttered, "Competing religions?" then "Untimely death?" Then he looked into Lamech-Cain's eyes and announced, "My father did not die."

Lamech-Cain twirled toward his sons. "Oh, my sons, I hope some day, when my mortal body leaves this fleeting world, that you will struggle just as mightily as Methuselah does with the passing of his father." Then he grasped an imaginary sword and declared, "And if my passing is by violent means, my sons, let you avenge the death of your father as well as Methuselah avenged the death of his."

Lamech-Cain rose from his throne, rushed forward, embraced Methuselah, and proclaimed, "This world is a better place because of you, Methuselah. My children, my city, and I are forever in your debt for ridding us of the curse of Cain and his stupid religion. No more will there be senseless human sacrifices from atop the Tower of Cain."

Methuselah glanced over at his sister, who was just shaking her head as Lamech-Cain continued. "Methuselah, I would like for you," then motioning toward Crista, "and your sister to be my guests tomorrow when I make the grand announcement about renaming the City of Cain."

Methuselah stared blankly, then asked, "You're going to rename the City of Cain?"

Lamech-Cain beamed. "But of course. We must rid the city of every vestige of the name of Cain, cleansing our city of the blood and ashes of thousands of victims of religious sacrifice. Let the name of Cain be never mentioned again."

Crista interrupted. Stressing his name, she stated, "Lamech-Cain, as much as we would like to stay in your city, Methuselah and I really must be going. We must hurry home to tell our mother that our father is gone."

"So humble, so noble," Lamech-Cain quickly replied. "Of course, please take your leave. Give my regards to your mother, and tell her how sorry I am for her husband's untimely passing."

Methuselah finally made a connection. "Uhh, Lamech-Cain, if you are going to erase the name of Cain from the city, what are you going to do about your name?"

"Ahh," Lamech-Cain responded, "a clever deduction. You really should visit my School of Humanism one day, Methuselah. You are a very bright man." He paused, then explained, "At the expense of possibly dishonoring my own father, I am forced to assume a new name." Then he turned to his sons and smiled. "I have discussed this matter at great length for many years with my children, in the event that I ever assumed control of the City of Cain. We decided that I should choose a name which befits the wisdom of man. Although the world does not know me by this name today, tomorrow the world shall know me as . . ."

As Lamech-Cain paused for effect, everyone in the room was startled when Crista blurted out the name: "Saaga."

Chapter Four

On the Way Home

"How did you know that?" Methuselah asked his sister as they made their way down the steps of Saaga's new mansion.

"I have my sources," Crista coolly replied.

"Wow! Did you see the stunned look on the faces of Saaga and his sons? You really caught them off guard, sis."

"Let's hurry out of the city before they come to their senses, big brother." As soon as they could, they were on their way out the south gate, headed toward home.

*   *   *   *

Once they were several miles into the countryside, Methuselah demanded an explanation. "How did you know that Lamech-Cain was going to change his name to Saaga? He said only his family knew."

Crista hurried along. "Let's make some decisions about our journey home, then I promise to tell you the whole story." And she did.

*   *   *   *

Each stop on the way home was similar, yet different. They first visited Meshach and Opal, Sarah's parents, who were overjoyed to see Crista, yet exceedingly sorrowful at the homegoing of Enoch and Arphaxad. "The world will never see the likes of those two again," Meshach sighed.

Meshach also encouraged Methuselah to take up his father's mantle. "Methuselah, it's part of the Lord's promises. God's Fourth Promise is that you will also preach unto the children of Adam." Methuselah hung his head in shame. "I am not my father, Grandpa." But Meshach was not easily dissuaded. "Methuselah, God did not call you to be your father. He called you to tell the world about your Heavenly Father."

*   *   *   *

The second stop was at Jared's homestead, where Enoch's parents warmly welcomed their long lost granddaughter. While Crista shared her story with Rachel, Jared invited Methuselah to take a walk out to the sheepcote.

Methuselah noticed that there was something different about his grandfather from what his father had told him. "I remember the day that your father went to Heaven, Methuselah." Methuselah did not understand. Jared wasn't there. "Methuselah, I was very disap-pointed when your father took up this prophet business. It was so extreme, almost radical, so very different from anything I ever knew." Methuselah nodded sympatheti-cally. "I understand, Grandpa. I felt the same way for many years."

Enoch's father continued. "For hundreds of years, I wished that your father would give up his foolishness and stay home and take care of his family and sheep." Methuselah nodded again. "Every time I thought of my son, a dark cloud appeared in my mind." Methuselah was wondering where Jared's thoughts were taking him.

"Two weeks ago, that dark cloud lifted. I saw for the first time that the spirit of Satan, the spirit of Cain, had clouded my mind to the truth that Enoch wasn't preaching foolishness, but rather the very Words of God." The old man hung his head in shame. "I was the fool, and I have led my family down the wrong path of ritual and religion for all our lives."

Methuselah gently put his arm around his grandfather. "Grandpa, I, too, was blinded for many years." With a lump in his throat, Methuselah offered, "Would you mind if I shared with you what I learned from Dad about the Words of God?"

Jared was eager, a little child searching for the truth. Methuselah explained how Satan had blinded the minds of Adam and Eve in the Garden of Eden, casting the world into sin, judgment, and death. But the Lord gave Adam and Eve the promise of the Redeemer, Who would one day redeem mankind from their sin. "And Grandpa, I will never forget the Seventh Promise which God gave to Enoch in the Garden of Eden: 'The Redeemer shall come in the fulness of time, and He shall be one of your descendants, Enoch.'"

Jared fell to his knees and looked up at his grandson. "Methuselah, that promise means that the Redeemer shall come through me, also?"

"That's right, Grandpa."

"How can I know the Redeemer?"

"Only through the eyes of faith, Grandpa. You must believe that God is, that He is a rewarder of them that diligently seek Him. Grandpa, you must place your faith in the coming Redeemer to save you from your sins."

Jared began to sob softly. "Is it really that simple, Methuselah?"

"Grandpa, the price for our salvation will be paid by the Redeemer, not by us."

"And so religion isn't just about ritual and sacrifice?"

"No, Grandpa, true religion isn't a ritual. It's a personal relationship with the Redeemer."

"Methuselah, can I have that personal relationship with the Redeemer?" And there, by the sheepcote, the new preacher led his first convert to the Lord.

Chapter Five

Stopover in Gom

The sun was going down as the two weary travelers approached the north gate of the City of Gom. "We'll never make it home tonight, Crista. We should spend the night with our friends."

Crista winced from a double curse. First of all, the closer she came to home, the stronger was her need to be reunited with her mother after being away for 240 years. Secondly, she became physically ill at the thought of spending the night in Gom, the place which lived in her nightmares for centuries. The sounds of Arphaxad's club swishing through the air and slamming into her father's head came back as if it had happened yesterday. Bile rose to her throat as she recalled the filth and stench of the thug's hair as she leaped and pounded on his back. But the worst memory, as she was kidnapped and driven away, was gazing into her brother's helpless eyes and crying out: "Pumpkinhead! Pumpkinhead! Help me, Pumpkinhead!"

"Are you all right, sis?" her brother asked.

"Oh, sure, Pumpkinhead," she calmly replied. "I was just thinking about a bad dream."

Methuselah wasn't sure what was going on inside his sister's head. All he could dream about was a hot meal and warm bed at Ludim and Perna's house.

Crista's mind rapidly switched tracks, recalling the time that the gallant blacksmith had kissed her hand on his front porch so long ago. As they opened the gate to his yard and walked up the path to Ludim's front door, Crista asked her brother: "Methuselah, do you think Ludim has heard about what happened at the Tower of Cain?"

Methuselah shrugged. "I don't know, sis. But news does travel pretty fast these days."

She then nudged her brother and asked another question: "Would you introduce me again to Ludim?"

As they stepped on the porch, Methuselah pondered the question. "Let me handle this. Step over to the side, sis." Then he knocked on the door.

From inside the house, they heard a loud grunt and robust voice: "Who in the world is out in the dark tonight?" Then he bellowed toward the door, "The blacksmith shop will open again in the morning!"

Methuselah was not so easily deterred from his dream of a hot meal and a warm bed. Pounding louder on the door, he tried to match bellow for bellow. "Will you open your door to an old friend?"

Immediately they heard a thrashing sound within and then footsteps stomping to the door. As the door opened, the beefy blacksmith gawked at his unexpected visitor. "Methuselah!" he shouted excitedly. As Ludim dashed out the door, Methuselah braced for the bear hug. Ludim did not disappoint. Then Ludim turned his head back toward the house and shouted, "Perna, Methuselah is home."

Methuselah winced as Ludim loosened his grip, then softened his tone. Almost gently, he said, "Son, I'm so sorry to hear about the death of your father."

Methuselah blinked his eyes, then struggled to free himself. "Ludim, if you invite me in for a hot meal, I will tell you all about it."

"Of course, boy, of course. My son-in-law is always welcome!" Turning his head back toward the house, he bellowed: "Get some hot soup on, Perna." As he swung his eyes back toward Enoch's son, Ludim caught a glimpse of someone else standing off to the side of his porch. He did a double take, switching his eyes between the man and the woman on his porch, wondering what his son-in-law was doing out at night with a strange lady. "Introduce me to your lady friend, Methuselah," Ludim pleaded.

As Ludim turned to look at the unknown lady, Methuselah quietly stated, "Ludim, this is my sister."

The blacksmith's face melted like heated clay as tears of joy poured down his cheeks at this unexpected good news. He spread his arms skyward and loudly proclaimed, "O God, You have kept Your promise!" Quick as a cat, he snatched Crista up in his arms, bawled like a baby, then through the sobs sputtered, "Crista, we'll never let you go again."

Methuselah coughed, then spoke up. "Uhh, Ludim, if you don't let go of my sister, I will never get my hot meal."

Ludim smiled, tenderly deposited his precious cargo back on the porch floor, and said, "Wait till Perna sees who's coming to dinner."

*   *   *   *

During a delicious dinner of barley soup, hot biscuits, and steaming apple cider, Ludim told the story that was being circulated around the known world about that fateful day at the Tower of Cain. Cain intended to kill the Prophet Enoch and his traveling companion Arphaxad at the Tower of Cain. However, during a scuffle, Zaava killed Arphaxad with a spear, Enoch threw Zaava off the Tower platform, and Cain killed Enoch with a spear. Finally, Methuselah used the staff of God to knock Cain off of the platform, thus ending the scuffle and the reign of the founder of the City of Cain and the cult of the Great Ebony Cow.

During much of Ludim's storytelling, Methuselah gulped his food and exclaimed, "No, that's not what happened at all." After eating several sugar cookies and settling down on a divan in the common room, Methuselah took a few minutes to explain what really happened. When he finished telling the tale, the blacksmith bellowed: "Methuselah, you must now take up your father's mantle and fulfill the Fourth Promise."

The timid shepherd just shook his head as three pairs of eyes looked into his soul. "You know, Grandpa Meshach and Adam said the same thing." Taking a deep breath, Methuselah insisted, "I don't think I can be a prophet like Dad was, but I guess I can tell people about the wonderful works of God."

Ludim reached over and pounded Methuselah on the back. "Attaboy, Methuselah. God can take a bucket of ore, melt it down in the heat, mold it in the furnace of affliction, strengthen it on the anvil of life's blows, and forge a shiny sword which God can wield to perform His wonderful works." Ludim stood and bowed. "God's going to use you in mighty ways, Methuselah. Mark my words."

"You make too much of this, Ludim," Methuselah mumbled. "I'm just a little fellow with a little faith."

"Exactly the kind of man God can use -- a humble man with a little faith in a big God!"

Then Methuselah told Ludim and Perna a very personal story of how God used him in a small way -- leading Jared to faith in the Redeemer.

"Glory be!" Ludim bellowed. "I have been praying for that old rascal for hundreds of years, right, Perna? Never give up, son. Never give up doing what God has called you to do."

Perna interrupted. "Methuselah, I want to hear more of your story and more of how you found Crista, but first, could you run an errand for me?"

The two house guests were perplexed. What kind of errand needed running in the dark of night in the City of Gom? She explained, "Please visit my youngest son. He's not taking the death of his wife very well." She paused, thinking of her deceased daughter, Methuselah's wife. "And Methuselah, you know what Tubal is going through."

*   *   *   *

As Methuselah grabbed another sugar cookie, Ludim insisted that he accompany Methuselah to Tubal's mansion. As they walked, Ludim gave

Methuselah the last two monthly reports from Lamech, Methuselah's only surviving child. After the thug Og murdered the rest of Lamech's family, Lamech took a one-year sabbatical from his position as the marketing director of Tubal Enterprises to hunt and kill Og. Lamech promised that he would send monthly progress reports.

It was Lamech's eighth report that changed everyone's life, the report that Adam was dying. Lamech's ninth and tenth reports were from overseas; he still had not found Og. "Ironic, isn't it?" Ludim said as he walked with Methuselah to Tubal's house. "Your son Lamech has spent nearly a year looking for Og, and yet you, Methuselah, have seen Og twice."

Methuselah pondered his friend's observations. "Hmmm," he spoke aloud. "I wonder how Lamech is going to take it when he finds out that I have seen Og twice, and yet Og still lives."

*   *   *   *

Something seemed different as the two men approached Tubal's mansion. "Ludim, the front door is open!"

"Tubal fired his butler, fired his whole staff."

As they reached the top of the steps, an unfamiliar stench insulted their nostrils. Methuselah peered inside. "What is that smell? I can't see a thing, Ludim. Why aren't any candles lit?"

"Nobody to light them." Ludim felt along the wall until he came to a candlestick. He struck a match, temporarily blinding the two men, then lit the candle.

As their eyes adjusted to the light, Methuselah was awestruck by the mess in the common room -- nearly every divan, table, and chair was chopped to pieces. As they moved carefully through the room, Methuselah's eyes zoomed toward the west wall -- the Great Ebony Cow was fallen, lying on its side, its head chopped off, the rest of its body hacked to pieces. Lying down next to the reclined cow lay the body of Tubal. "Is he dead, Ludim?"

Ludim just shook his head. "Dead drunk."

"Drunk!?!" Methuselah exclaimed. "Drunk what?"

"A new drink developed in the pits of hell and birthed in the kitchens of the City of Cain -- wine."

"Wine? What's that? Never heard of it."

"Something fouler than eating meat, my friend."

Methuselah pinched his nose. "It smells dreadful, worse than a pickling solution."

"That's what wine does to your brain."

"Why would anyone want to pickle their brain?"

"To deaden the pain, to deaden the memories, to shorten their life, to ruin their family, to destroy lives and civilization."

Just then, Tubal let out a loud belch and squinted his eyes. After hiccuping, he slurred his first words of the day. "Why, if it isn't Methuselah the Mighty Cain Killer." After hiccuping again, he challenged: "Go ahead! Kill me like you killed Cain." Then he began to sob. "Go ahead," he sniffled, "kill me like your father killed my wife." Then he lowered his head, sprawled out on the floor, and bawled uncontrollably.

*   *   *   *

Methuselah did not know what to say. He looked down at the pitiful figure on the floor, then back at Tubal's father. Ludim took a deep breath, walked over to his son, and with great effort, lifted him into the only remaining chair. While Methuselah stood helpless, Ludim took the candle, disappeared into the kitchen, then came back out in just a few moments with a bucket of water. Before Methuselah's incredulous eyes, Ludim poured the bucket of water over his son's head.

Tubal sputtered and flailed his arms. "Leave me alone!" he screamed. "Leave me alone!" As Tubal hung his head, Ludim reached over and lifted his chin. "Son, all Methuselah wants to do is tell you what really happened at the Tower of Cain."

The son swatted his father's arm away and spat on him. "I already know what happened. My wife is dead!" Then he turned his gaze toward Methuselah and sneered: "Can you bring her back to life?" As Methuselah shook his head, Tubal begged: "You can't do anything for me, except kill me. Kill me with the staff of God, now!"

Methuselah did not know what to say, except to say that he knew what it was like to lose his wife and that he was sorry. He paused, then gently said, "Perhaps I could come back at a better time."

Tubal stared at him vacantly, then reached under the table for a bottle. After taking a long swig, he belched again and fell off the chair. Sprawled on the floor, he clutched the bottle to his heart and started crying out his wife's name: "Zaava. Zaava."

Methuselah lowered his head and covered his eyes. He knew then that he would have to preach against wine, just as his father had to oppose meat eating. Ludim walked over, grabbed a curtain, placed it over his fallen son, then led Methuselah through the litter to the front door. "Well, Ludim, old friend," Methuselah said, "I wasn't much help in there tonight."

Ludim clutched at his heart. "Nothing can help Tubal tonight, except the Lord."

Chapter Six

The Final Leg Home

That evening, before bed, Crista briefly related her story to Ludim and Perna, from the time of her kidnapping in the City of Gom to the time of Adam's death. The hearts of the older couple were touched to hear that Adam had a vision of Enoch and Arphaxad, as well as Eve and Abel, in Heaven. "Children, you are going to see your father again."

Methuselah bowed his head. "I know what you're thinking, Methuselah," Perna added. "We live with the same thought every day. We miss our little girl Martha, but one day, we will see her again."

As Crista moved to comfort her brother, Ludim mentioned another loved one in Heaven. "Crista, I'm sure that Methuselah has filled you in on all of the happenings here in Gom during the last two hundred and forty years." As she nodded her head, Ludim softly spoke, "We are going to see Adah's little girl in Heaven, too."

Crista struggled for breath and closed her eyes as memories of her childhood friend Adah flooded over her. Poor Adah! Entranced by the city lights, she fell victim to the clutches of Zaava, became a temple prostitute, and gave birth out of wedlock to a little girl sacrificed at the dedication of the Temple of Gom. Although the loss of her daughter led Adah to break the bondage of sin and trust in the Redeemer, she was convinced that God had cursed her womb. After nearly eighty years of marriage to Arphaxad, the couple had never conceived a child.

* * * *

Crista's thoughts were interrupted by Ludim's gentle voice. "I am sure that you two want to get an early start in the morning." The two weary travelers nodded their heads as Ludim continued. "Let me mention just two more things before you get some well-deserved bed rest. First, as far as I know, the news of the passing of your father and Arphaxad has not yet reached your family."

Methuselah let out a long whistle. "I guess I'm gonna have to tell Momma." He reached over and grasped his sister's hand.

Ludim wasn't done. "And listen carefully. Methuselah, you remember that Elihu stayed with your mother while you journeyed to see Adam."

"Sure," Methuselah replied. "Elihu stayed to take care of the sheep."

At the mention of Elihu's name, Crista jerked. She remembered Adah's older brother, a soft-spoken, steady young man, a little older than herself. Before she knew it, the words came tumbling out of her mouth: "Did Elihu ever marry?" Perna knew the thought behind Crista's question, but Ludim was oblivious.

"Well, Methuselah," Ludim continued, "a young, single fellow such as Elihu could not very well stay alone with your mother, so Adah stayed with them, also."

"Ahh," Methuselah realized, "I also have to tell Adah that she, too, is now a widow." As he rubbed his eyes, he pondered, "I look forward to taking Crista home tomorrow, but I don't look forward to being the bearer of bad news."

"Just be careful, lad," the blacksmith warned, "when you tell Adah about her husband's passing. Make sure she is sitting, or even better, lying down." Methuselah looked quizzically at Ludim, wondering what he meant, not understanding why tears were swelling up in the blacksmith's eyes. "You see," Ludim explained, "Arphaxad never knew that he was going to be a father."

                    *   *   *   *

Before the first rays of sunlight peeked over the city walls, Ludim was hitching his horse to the wagon while Perna was serving hot biscuits, butter, and honey to the two well rested travelers. After a prayer for travel mercies, a sweet homecoming, and Adah and her baby, Ludim led his horse and wagon through the gate and out into the street. Perna told brother and sister to come by again soon to visit; and then the horse headed south through the main street of Gom.

Warehouses gave way to businesses until the wagon reached the marketplace. "Stop, Methuselah!" Crista blurted. She pointed to a spot in the marketplace and said, "That's where Arphaxad clubbed Daddy, and that's where he tied me onto his horse." Methuselah winced, never enjoying those memories of one of his greatest failures. Crista noticed, and told her brother:

"Now look, brother, both of us are back here, alive and well. We must put that day behind us, do you hear?"

Methuselah winced again. His sister was right. He had failed before, and he would surely fail again; but he must go on, looking forward, not behind. "You're right, sis. Let's go on."

Then she smiled. "Well," she retorted, "before we go on, show me where the Temple of Gom stood."

Methuselah looked around. "Well, sis, I never really saw it. I wasn't there that day when Dad, Arphaxad, and Ludim raced into Gom trying to save Adah's baby."

Crista was insistent. "Can't you tell me anything about the temple?"

Methuselah rubbed his jaw. "Lemme see. Uhhh, Dad said that the temple was right in the middle of the main street, next to the city fountain." Pointing in that direction, he remembered how his father described it. "It was a square building, thirty feet high, with six pillars on each side. And on the east side of the temple was one of those silly black ebony cows." His chuckle quickly turned to a frown. "And right in the middle of the temple, there was a brazen altar."

Crista looked at the fountain and surrounding area, trying to imagine what it must have looked like. "Aren't there any remains?"

Methuselah chuckled again. "Not much remains after nearly two hundred and twenty years." And then he shuddered. "And don't forget what happened to the temple. After Dad gave an invitation to Adah, Aram, and everybody else to escape from the destruction to come, the ground began to rumble, crack, split, and divide. Then a great flame shot forty feet into the sky, surrounding the temple."

"It must have been a horrible sight," Crista shuddered.

"Then, the ground began to sink, the pillars of the temple began to crack and topple, and then, with an awful gulp, the earth swallowed the ruins of the Temple of Gom, and all who remained inside."

"Including Uncle Aram?" his sister asked.

"Including Uncle Aram," Methuselah sighed. "What an awful waste of a young life."

Crista looked over the now peaceful scene of an earlier devastation. "You know, brother, that could have been you and me in the Temple of Gom."

Methuselah nodded his head. "There go I, but for the grace of God."

*   *   *   *

As Ludim's horse led the wagon through the south gate and into the countryside toward home, Crista asked her brother where his homestead had been. Without looking in that direction, he pointed vaguely and replied, "Several valleys southwest of here."

She bit her lip, then asked, "Do you want to drive by there this morning and show me?"

Methuselah kept his head down. "Nothing to see. Everything I built, and nearly everyone I loved, burned up."

As a tear rolled down her brother's cheek, Crista leaned over, touched her brother's hands holding the reins, then clenched his right shoulder. Without saying another word, they drove in silence for a while, each lost in private thoughts.

*   *   *   *

Crista spoke up first, pointing to the trees alongside the road. "Methuselah, those cedars look taller than I remember."

"Well, I guess so, sis. You haven't seen them for two hundred and forty years."

She thought back to a time much earlier. "Do you remember on which day God created trees?"

Methuselah tried to remember some of the earliest Tales of Father Adam, no, the Words of God. "Uhh, lemme see. The, uhh, hmmm, uhh, the fourth day?"

"Nope," she exclaimed, "the third day. 'And the earth brought forth grass, and herb yielding seed after his kind, and the tree yielding fruit, whose seed was in itself, after his kind: and God saw that it was good. And the evening and the morning were the third day.'"

Methuselah glanced over at his sister. "Kinda impressive. I never remembered you very much interested in trees and stuff. Last I recall, you were more interested in the things of the city."

His sister laughed. "I had my fill of the city in just one day, brother. God's nature is much more interesting."

Methuselah chuckled. "My sister the nature lover. Who would have ever thought?" After riding for several hours, they neared Enoch's homestead. "Look," Crista exclaimed, "there's the tamarisk grove. It's still there."

Chapter Seven

Finally Home

Sarah could not remember the last time she had felt this lonely. Adah was in the house every day of course, but all Adah could do was moan and vomit. Neither of Sarah's pregnancies had been so hard. At times the thought of the curse of Adah's womb flashed through Sarah's mind, but she always quickly banished such morbid thoughts. She knew in her heart that God was going to bless Adah and Arphaxad with a beautiful baby. But apparently, until that day, Adah would not be much of a companion.

And Elihu spent most of his time in the hills with the sheep. And even when he was home, he was too quiet and too polite. He could sit in the common room all evening long and never say a word. She wiped a tear from her eye as she thought of how gabby her little girl had been. For the ten thousandth time, she wondered if she would ever see her daughter again.

And why was it taking her husband, her son, and Arphaxad so long to return from their trip to Adam's homestead? Was Adam's life lingering? Did they run into trouble? Would she ever see them again?

Of course they would return, she scolded herself. They always had before, and they always would. No, that wasn't true. Someday, her husband wouldn't return. But whenever that thought flashed through her mind, she always quickly buried it.

She walked outside and looked up the dogwood-lined path leading up to the tamarisk grove. Elihu and the sheep were expected back later in the day. The only sound she could hear was Adah throwing up in her bedroom. "I have to get out of this house!" she thought.

Sarah strolled over to the herb garden and spotted the weeds that had taken advantage of her diligent nursing of Adah. She pointed at one rather large weed and spoke out loud: "Your time is up, Mr. Weed." Then she chuckled at the ridiculousness of talking to a weed. "I'm too lonely," she told herself.

She walked over to the weed, grabbed it by the stem, and yanked hard. Only half of the weed came up in her hand. Some weeds don't die easy, she thought. She walked over to the shed, grabbed a spade, and returned to the garden. Digging down, she plucked up the root. "Goodbye, Mr. Weed," she exulted, starting a new pile of dead weeds.

As she then looked at all of the other weeds, Sarah thought, Why do the weeds grow back every year? She plopped down in the middle of her herb garden and pouted: "Here I am, suffering from God's curse on Eve and God's curse on Adam." She felt sorry for herself. "Why isn't Enoch here to help me pull out the thorns and thistles? Why isn't Methuselah here to help me?" And then a tear came to her eye. "Why isn't Crista here to help me?"

*   *   *   *

Just then, Sarah heard a neigh. Sitting in the herb garden, she turned her head to look up to the top of the hill. A horse and wagon were just pulling into view. She started to yell out, "Company coming!" then realized that Elihu wasn't home to hear and Adah would only hear her between the heaves. I wonder who's visiting, she thought. Then she had an excited thought. Maybe the men are home.

The wagon stopped in the shade of the tamarisks, and she couldn't identify who was in the wagon. Her hope of Enoch's homecoming was quickly stifled when she discerned that one of the persons in the wagon was wearing a dress. Well, she thought, maybe I won't have a lonely afternoon.

Just as she was prepared to stand up, the two people stepped down from the wagon. Even in the shade, she recognized the gait of the man. "My son is home." And then a dagger pierced her heart. "Where's Enoch? Where's Arphaxad?"

*   *   *   *

Before she could move or utter a sound, she saw her son do the most remarkable thing. He took the strange woman's hand in his. Sarah gasped. Her son had never touched another woman since his beloved Martha died; he had sworn that he would never re-marry. Yet, who was this strange woman appearing with him on the hill overlooking her home? Then she watched as her son wrapped his right arm around the woman's shoulder and drew her close to him.

Sarah was stunned. Where was Enoch? Who was this strange woman? Why would her son treat this strange woman with such familiarity? Why, the only women he would ever hug would be his mother or his . . .

*   *   *   *

The word caught in Sarah's throat. As the couple on the hill moved out of the shadows into the light, Sarah saw the brown hair flowing in the wind. "It can't be!" she cried. Then, "It must be." She jumped to her feet and cried out to the person she had longed to speak to for over two hundred years: "CRISTA!"

Her daughter heard her name across the small valley. She looked down the hill, spotted her mother in the herb garden, and cried back: "MOMMA!"

*   *   *   *

Methuselah could not hold back his sister, and no force on Earth could hold back Sarah. As they flew into each other's arms, as Methuselah tried in vain to hold back his tears, he slowly walked down the path toward his mother and sister, stopping only when the front door opened. Into the sunlight stepped pale and gaunt Adah, wondering what all the yelling was about. She first saw Methuselah, alone. Then she spotted Sarah, hugging some strange woman. Sarah turned to face her patient. "Crista's home."

Adah stood there befuddled. Crista's home? Methuselah's home? But where is my husband? Then

she knew. The father of her child was not coming home.
Adah crumpled into a heap on the porch.

Methuselah quickly carried Adah into the
common room and gently laid her on one of the divans.
Sarah dashed into the courtyard and wet a dishrag while
Crista knelt to hold Adah's hand. When Sarah returned
and soothed Adah's forehead, she quickly recovered. As
she looked into the eyes of the three people around her,
Adah asked the same question that Sarah was asking:
"My husband isn't coming home, is he?"

Crista squeezed Adah's hand as Methuselah
grabbed his mother and held her tight. No words were
exchanged, only tears.

Chapter Eight

"Daddy Never Died!"

Remarkably, Adah's health improved from that moment. The shock of losing her husband calmed her body down sufficiently to stop the frequent upheavals in her stomach. She asked Crista to get her a cup of water, and before Crista could return from the courtyard, Adah was already sitting up by herself. After taking a few sips, she raised herself from the divan, placed her cup of water on the eating table, and then hugged her long lost childhood friend. Stepping back, placing her hands on Crista's shoulders, and looking into Crista's still teary eyes, Adah wiped the tears from her eyes and smiled: "I can't believe you are back home, Crista. I want to hear your whole story." She paused, then continued. "But first, I want to hear every detail of how my husband died."

Sarah then broke away from her son's embrace and wrapped her arms around dear Adah. Both of the widows stood there sobbing for several minutes. Crista and Methuselah silently left them alone and walked into the courtyard. "Hey, sis," Methuselah suggested, "why don't you put some lunch together while I put away Ludim's horse and wagon." Crista hugged her brother. "Men! Even at a time like this, all you can think about is food."

Several minutes later, Crista brought a light lunch of salad, day old bread, and butter into the common room. Sarah and Adah both offered to set the table, and by the time Methuselah returned inside, lunch was ready, and the ladies were seated at the table. As Methuselah walked through the door, Adah looked up and asked, "Did my husband die peacefully?"

Methuselah smiled. "Adah, I can honestly say that your husband died the most peaceful and the most glorious death that any man shall ever witness." She slumped over in her chair and began to softly sob. After several moments, she demanded, "Every detail. Don't leave out one detail. Someday, I want to tell my husband's child how his father died."

Sarah wiped a tear from her eye and asked hesitantly, "Methuselah, were Enoch and Arphaxad together when, you know, when they . . . died?"

Methuselah sighed, walked over to his mother, put his arm around her shoulder, and answered, "Dad and Arphaxad were together at the end, and I can honestly and happily say that I watched both of them leave Earth for Heaven." As tears of joy started to fall from Sarah's eyes, Methuselah made one further statement. "But Mom, I must honestly and happily say that Dad did not die peacefully."

Sarah, perplexed by her son's words, turned her head and stared up at him. "What!?! You're happy that your father didn't die peacefully?"

Methuselah shrugged. "Mom, you won't believe this, but Daddy never died!"

Sarah blinked, then blinked again. "Lunch can wait," she declared. "Son, do you mind explaining that last statement?" As Methuselah started to explain, Sarah repeated Adah's demand, "And remember, every detail. Don't leave out one detail."

*   *   *   *

Methuselah started his story with the three men climbing the stairway to the temple on top of the Tower of Cain. Adah even laughed when Methuselah described her husband's fear of heights. She laughed again at Arphaxad's response when Enoch told him that God was with them: "Along with fifty guards, Cain, Zaava, and Og."

Sarah gasped. "Og was there?" She closed her eyes and saw the gravestones near the tamarisk grove overlooking Enoch's homestead. "Yes, Mom," Methuselah explained, "Og was there at our capture at Adam's homestead, and Og was there for our execution at the City of Cain." All Sarah could think was how disappointed her grandson Lamech would be that he was not there to avenge the death of his mother and brothers and sisters. Her mind came back to the present as Adah persisted, "Every detail at the Tower of Cain, Methuselah."

"OK! OK!" he replied. He went on to explain how the guards led the three men to the edge of the platform overlooking the flaming pit. "Mom, I'm afraid your son was not very brave and bold. When I looked down at the flaming pit two hundred feet below, I gagged."

Adah piped up. "I can relate to that."

"Well, ladies," Methuselah continued, "I backed away from the edge of the pit, got down on my knees, and vomited."

Adah added, "I can relate to that, too."

*   *   *   *

Methuselah then explained how his father stood up to Cain, even preaching one final message from atop the Tower of Cain to the hundred thousand people below. Then, he asked the ladies if they could handle the details of exactly how Arphaxad died. All three silently nodded their head. When Methuselah got to the part of the story where Zaava was chosen by Cain to be Enoch's executioner, Adah stood up. "I can't hear any more sitting at the table." She pushed her chair back, ran her hands through her hair, then suggested, "Why don't we ladies sit together on one of the divans." Without any further suggestion, the three ladies sat on the divan, Crista in the middle, with one arm around her mother and her other arm around Adah. "OK," Crista sighed, "I think we're ready."

Adah added, "Every detail. Don't leave out one detail."

*   *   *   *

Methuselah stood in front of the divan and acted out the story as best he could. When he acted out how Arphaxad died, Adah lifted her head and sighed deeply as Sarah asked incredulously, "That's what you call a peaceful death, dying with a spear in your chest atop the Tower of Cain?"

"Mom," her son countered, "I wouldn't have believed it if I hadn't been there." He described the bolt of light, the booming sound, and finally the bright, misty, swirling cloud -- the glory of God -- descending from Heaven and enveloping the two friends on the platform.

Methuselah took a deep breath. "I could see inside the cloud. I could see Daddy looking up to Heaven, thanking God, then I watched as he looked again at his friend."

"And, and, . . ." Adah persisted.

"Arphaxad opened his eyes."

Adah leaned back, gasped, and fainted.

*   *   *   *

Sarah ran to the courtyard to get some fresh water and a wet cloth while Crista stretched her friend out on the divan. All Methuselah could do was say, "I'm sorry."

After a few minutes, Adah was reviving. Sarah and Crista helped her sit up, then Adah asked if she could get some fresh air. After walking around the front yard for a minute, Adah asked if she and the other ladies could sit on the porch while Methuselah finished telling his incredible tale. Seated, Adah took a deep breath and asked, "What happened next?"

Methuselah described the voice of God, and how Arphaxad's body stood erect, and how Arphaxad grasped the spear protruding from his chest, pulled it out, and raised it high over his head. "When Arphaxad dropped his spear to the platform below, Cain grabbed it, turned toward the swirling mist, and shouted, 'You shall not escape me, Enoch.' Then he launched the spear straight toward Daddy's heart."

Sarah flinched, then listened as her son explained how the spear struck the swirling mist, spun round and round, faster and faster, then launching straight back toward Cain, struck him in the heart. Methuselah acted out how Cain dropped the staff of God as he struggled to take the spear out of his chest. "That was my opportunity," Methuselah added.

"Opportunity to do what?" Sarah queried.

"Well," he explained, "I was still fighting off my dizziness and waves of nausea. I saw the staff of God there. I told myself, Use the staff of God to help yourself stand up. So I crawled toward the staff, grabbed one end, and started to get up. Just then, Cain looked down, grabbed the other end of the staff, and started pulling."

Sarah's eyes were big. "You engaged in a tug of war with Cain over the staff of God?"

"Mom," he explained, "I was so weak. All I wanted to do was get up. I needed that staff. So when Cain started tugging on it, I tugged back."

Adah's eyes grew big. "You defeated Cain in a tug of war?"

Methuselah shrugged. "Hey, it was no big thing. Cain had a spear sticking through his heart. I could see his blood spurting out everywhere. He lost his grip, stumbled backward, and slipped, I think, on his own blood and my vomit." As Adah's stomach turned, Methuselah acted out how Cain teetered on the edge of the platform, cried out "I shall never die!" then toppled over the edge, screaming all the way down to the flaming pit below.

Crista commented, "Cain was not immortal after all. He fell into his own pit."

Adah recalled her daughter again and Cain's role in her daughter's murder. She uttered softly, "Justice has been done. Blessed be the name of the Lord."

As Methuselah described watching the swirling mist rising into the sky with its Heaven bound pilgrims, Adah and Sarah started to sob. When Sarah reached over and touched Adah's shoulder, Adah sniffled, "I miss him so much." Sarah's own grief was just as fresh. "I know."

The two widows clung to each other, and Adah sniffled again. "Sarah, I'm so happy for you. I'm so happy that your daughter has finally come home. But Sarah," Adah cried, "my daughter can never come home!" As she sobbed, Sarah stroked her hair and whispered, "Dear Adah, one day you will travel to her home, and your daughter and your husband will be waiting there for you." As she let out a deep breath, Adah softly uttered, "Blessed be the name of the Lord."

Part Two

The Last Two Hundred and Forty Years

700 A.C. to 940 A.C.

Chapter Nine

Kidnapped!

The next sound that they heard was the bleating of sheep. Elihu was back.

Methuselah encouraged the ladies to go back inside and rest, or if they so decided, make a hot meal for the returning shepherd. Then he bounded up the hill to meet his best friend and break the news about Enoch and Arphaxad.

Some time later, the front door to Enoch's common room opened. Elihu peered inside, smelled some soup, and then saw Sarah with her arm around his sister. When she saw her brother, Adah leaped up and ran to him, burying her face into his chest. He stroked her hair and gently said, "I'm so sorry, sis. I'm so sorry."

They stood that way for several minutes. Then Sarah stood and started walking toward the courtyard; Elihu unexpectedly dashed to her and gave her a big hug. "Sarah," he said, as tears were rolling down his cheeks, "I'm so sorry about your husband. He was the greatest man I have ever known."

Sarah sighed and smiled up at him. "Thank you, Elihu. You are so kind."

As he released Enoch's wife, the next unexpected thing happened. Another woman, a beautiful woman with green eyes, brown hair, and unblemished skin, appeared in the doorway to the courtyard. As their eyes met, a confused look spread across Elihu's face. He turned to look at Sarah and mumbled, "I'm sorry, Sarah. I didn't know you had a visitor."

Sarah smiled. "Oh, Elihu, this young lady is no visitor. My daughter is finally home."

Elihu grabbed his chest and leaned against the table. CRISTA!?! He couldn't believe it. The girl, no, the woman that he had prayed for for two hundred and forty years was now suddenly standing in front of him. And she was more beautiful, more radiant, than he had ever dreamed. His breath was taken away. He knew that he looked like a fool and smelled like a shepherd. He couldn't move. He couldn't talk. Then he thought to himself that he should be ashamed. He was looking at this lovely woman this way, and she had just lost her father. He wanted to say something, anything, but his lips wouldn't move.

His embarrassment was increased as she walked toward him. He thought again, for the one hundred thousandth time, how he longed to hold her in his arms. And here she was, walking toward him. He almost backed away, and then she stuck out her right hand. As she reached for his limp right hand, she said in the most melodious voice, "It is so good to see you again after all these years, Elihu."

Elihu finally got a grip on himself, and he firmly grasped Crista's hand. Putting his left hand on top of their handshake, he marveled at the baby-like smoothness of her skin. He opened his mouth and blurted out, "Oh, Crista, it is so good to see you, too." Then, feeling suddenly too familiar, he lapsed back into his normal formality. "I am so sorry to hear about your father."

Then Crista put her left hand on top of his. His skin tingled as it had never tingled before as she replied, "And I am so sorry about your brother-in-law."

Just then, Methuselah entered the common room and sensed sparks flying at the other end of the room as he noticed Elihu holding hands with his sister. He couldn't believe his ears when he heard taciturn Elihu ardently declare to Crista: "I want to hear about everything that has happened to you."

Neither Sarah nor Adah could believe their ears either. Normally, Elihu could sit all evening in the common room without saying a word. Sarah decided that it was time to interrupt their conversation. "Elihu, all of us want to hear Crista's story. But first, why don't you clean up and change into something fresh." That sounded like a good idea to Elihu, who was suddenly uncomfortable smelling like a sheep. Sarah continued, "Meanwhile, I'll get some spare bedrooms ready and the other ladies can finish getting dinner ready." That sounded like an even better idea.

*   *   *   *

Elihu picked at his hot lentil soup, fresh salad, fresh fruit, and bread during the dinner. He tried not to be obvious, but everyone except Crista was keenly aware that Elihu had a hard time keeping his eyes off of her. After the dishes were cleared away and washed, they all retired to the common room. Adah and Elihu sat arm in arm on one divan, and Methuselah sat with his arm around his mother on another divan. Crista turned one of the eating table chairs around and faced her listeners. "Now, Crista," her mother declared, "tell us what has happened to you during the last two hundred and forty years."

Adah added, "Every detail. Don't leave out one detail."

Crista laughed. "We'll be here until next year if I do that."

Methuselah spoke up. "Just tell the story in your own words, sis."

Crista wondered, "Where do I begin?"

Elihu answered, "Start with the kidnapping in 700 A.C."

So she did.

*   *   *   *

"Adah, you remember, as little girls, how excited we were about the big city. I couldn't wait to get there on the day that Daddy drove Methuselah and me to the City of Gom. Methuselah pointed out the city gate, the gong, the marketplace, and the fountain. I remember, when we reached the fountain, how Methuselah and I argued over who would get water for Otto the ox. Oh, by the way, whatever happened to Otto?"

Sarah replied tersely. "He went the way of all flesh, except apparently Enoch's, long ago. Now, get on with your story."

Crista smiled and continued. "I remember how I was going to slap Ludim if he tried to give me a hug like he did Methuselah when they last visited the city. But then, Ludim surprised me by gallantly kissing my hand. Like Daddy said then, I was speechless.

I was so eager to get to the marketplace that I didn't listen to a word that Daddy and Ludim talked about, though I recalled later Ludim talking about thugs, big men, evil men, armed with swords and clubs. When we drove to the marketplace, Methuselah and I were playfully fighting over the last of Perna's homemade sugar cookies. You know, those were the last sugar cookies I ate for over two hundred years."

Her audience dropped their jaws. "Where in the world did you live, Crista?" her mother asked.

"Momma, I'll get to that later. Anyway, Daddy parked the wagon in the marketplace and then led Otto back to Ludim's stable. Methuselah stayed in the wagon like Daddy said, but I jumped out after Daddy was out of sight and started looking at all of the beautiful things in the other stalls. More and more vendors showed up, and I had more and more stuff to look at, and I felt like I was in Heaven. Boy, was I ever wrong!

Customers started flocking to the marketplace, and I gawked at all of the strange people. I just knew I wanted to spend the rest of my life in such an exciting place. But then, everything changed when a horse and wagon drove into the marketplace. I was several booths away when I first saw those three ugly men. Their wagon stopped right in front of our stall."

Sarah was appalled. "Those men came right to your stall, Crista?"

"That's right, Momma. I later learned that our stall was their chosen destination. I remember seeing the biggest, ugliest thug jump out of the wagon right in front of Methuselah, who was sitting in our wagon seat. The big, ugly guy . . ."

Adah interrupted. "Crista, do you mind just calling the big, ugly guy by his name?"

Crista nodded. "Sure. Anyways, Arphaxad patted Methuselah on the head and asked him a question."

Methuselah playfully explained. "The big, ugly guy asked me if he could look at a bundle of wool."

Crista asked, "What did you tell him, brother?"

He answered, "I told him to wait until my father returned."

Crista continued. "So, the next thing I saw, the big, uhh, Arphaxad walked to the side of the wagon and picked up a bundle. I could see Methuselah rise to stop him, but Arphaxad just swatted Methuselah with the back of his hand."

Sarah gasped and looked at her son. "I never knew that, Methuselah."

Her son just shook his head. "Mom, it was a really bad day."

"I wasn't going to let anyone slap my brother around, so I dashed to our booth and yelled at Arphaxad, 'Put that bundle down, you bully!'"

Elihu commented, "That was very brave, Crista."

"Well, I guess I have never liked bullies. Arphaxad turned around and smiled. 'What do we have here?' Then he held the bundle of wool over his head, and dared me to get it. 'Jump, little pony, jump!' And I did. Every time he would lower the bundle, I would jump for it. 'Give that back to me, you thug!' I shrieked. 'Wait until my father gets here.' Arphaxad kept taunting me. 'Jump higher, my little pony.'

And all of a sudden, I heard Daddy's voice. 'Put the bundle down, you thug!' Arphaxad lowered the bundle as he turned to face Daddy. Well, you know me. I grabbed that bundle, jerked it away from that thug, and tossed it up to Methuselah. I remember Dad and Arphaxad getting into an argument and Arphaxad threatening to take away his little girl."

"Were you frightened, Crista?" Elihu pleaded.

"Nah, not then. I knew my Daddy could take on anybody. But then those other two thugs sneaked up behind Daddy and pinned his arms. Arphaxad walked over to his wagon, pulled out a hard shittim club, and walked over in front of Daddy, who was still defiant. 'You spineless, brainless thug!' he said. Sorry, Adah. 'Why don't you stand and fight me like a man?'

It was one of the worst sights I have ever seen in my life. That thug twirled his club, smiled, and said, 'Let's see who will stand.' He reared back, swung that club, and landed a blow just below Daddy's kneecap. Daddy dropped to his knees in agony, but didn't cry out. Then Arphaxad yelled to the gathering crowd in the marketplace, 'Let us now see who is brainless!' That thug swung his club one more time, clobbered Daddy in the head, and sent him flying across the street."

As she paused telling the story, Crista noticed that both of the other women were crying. Sarah finally spoke up. "That was the worst day of my life, but at least Arphaxad knocked some sense into my husband's head."

Adah sniffled. "Thanks for saying that, Sarah."

Methuselah's mind was reliving that day. "I was too stunned to move, but Crista let out a bloodcurdling yell, leaped on Arphaxad's back, and started pounding on him."

Crista continued.   "Lot of good that did. Arphaxad just grabbed me, took me over to his wagon, threw me over his horse, tied me down, hopped in his wagon, and drove south out of town."

Her brother interrupted. "Don't forget your last words to me, Crista."

She smiled at her brother.   "Pumpkinhead! Pumpkinhead! Help me, Pumpkinhead!"

Chapter Ten

Slave Trade

Elihu's heart was breaking. "Crista, that must have been the worst day of your life."

She shook her head. "Sadly, no. It only got worse."

Sarah grabbed her heart. "Wait a minute. I have got to take a break." Everyone took a few minutes to refill their cups and take care of some personal matters; then all of them reconvened in the common room. Sarah sighed, chuckled, and said, "Well, Crista, now that we have heard the good part of your story, why don't you start telling us about the bad part."

Adah added, "You know, Arphaxad never told me much of the details of what happened next. I think he was too ashamed."

Elihu was torn between his fondness for Crista and for his old friend Arphaxad. "I think you are right, sis. You know, after all the hours I spent nursing him after he was wounded and after he was redeemed, he never wanted to talk much about his sinning days."

"Well," Crista said, continuing her story, "I remember bouncing along the road, feeling like every joint in my body was going to come loose. Arphaxad whipped his horse unmercifully for several miles."

Elihu interrupted. "Crista, did he ever whip you?"

Crista let out a deep breath. "Actually, no. In fact, believe it or not, Arphaxad was very gentle and tender with me."

Elihu was astonished. "He was!?! I was afraid that, uhh, he and the other thugs, uhh, would have, uhh, abused you."

Crista continued, "That was the surprising thing. Any time that the other two thugs got near me during the whole trip, Arphaxad would warn them, 'Leave her alone, boys. We'll get more if we leave her untouched.'"

Elihu was indignant. "And what did he mean by that?"

"Hold on, Elihu," she answered. "I'm coming to that. When they finally stopped, they pulled off the road and rested their horses. They stuffed me in a bag, gagged my mouth, . . ."

"Here! Here!" her brother joked.

Crista ignored him. ". . . and laid me in the back of the wagon. Then, when the sun went down, they changed clothes, put on hooded cloaks, and headed north back toward the City of Gom."

Adah figured it out. "Ahh, I see. By riding south, they were trying to deceive any pursuers. Their real destination was the City of Cain?"

"Correct, Adah," Crista said. "They slipped through the south gate of Gom, moved quietly through the city, and out the north gate. Then they trotted their horses slowly and carefully through the night. Each stage of the trip, Arphaxad had fresh horses to make his trip go as fast as possible. They only stopped to feed me and let me relieve myself. They wanted me to be in good shape when we reached the City of Cain.

After many days, we arrived in the City of Cain. That's when they took me out of the bag and ungagged me, but they still left my hands and feet bound. Although I marveled at the size and beauty of the city, the thrill was gone. All I wanted to do was escape, make my way back home, and live the rest of my life in the peace and quiet of the country."

"What happened in the City of Cain, Crista?" Elihu asked.

"Arphaxad drove straight to the slave market."

Sarah shuddered. She remembered the horrible story of how Arphaxad and his thugs had later started a slave market in the City of Gom, how they had paraded naked slaves at the city gate, how Methuselah's wife Martha, as a twelve-year-old, had nearly been sold there except for the intervention of God and Sarah's husband. She commented: "You're right, Crista. Your story is getting worse."

As Sarah rubbed her eyes, Crista continued. "As Arphaxad reached the slave market, he waved to another man leaving in a large wagon. He was tall, like Arphaxad, but not as heavy."

Adah jested: "Was he as ugly?"

Crista smiled. "Yes, well, no, I mean I couldn't tell very well at first. He wasn't filthy, like Arphaxad, but he had a black beard, like your husband. But this other man's beard was neatly trimmed, and his hair, though too long for my taste, was, well, unlike Arphaxad's, manageable. His most peculiar feature was his eyes. His right eye was a bright green, but his left eye was a cold gray."

Elihu coughed. "You seemed to have taken a particular interest in this one fellow, Crista."

"You'll understand in a moment," she replied, ignoring any intent in his question. "I noticed that the driver and his three men all wore daggers on their hips, their left hip. And laying on the wagon seat next to the driver was a sword, a long sword, a very shiny, sharp looking sword. Then I noticed in the back of his large wagon a number of bags like the one I had been in. And most of those bags were moving. The other man reined his horse to a stop and held a brief conversation with Arphaxad. The man looked very upset about something. I didn't know then if he was upset with Arphaxad or with something else. The next thing I know, Arphaxad motioned to his two friends to stuff me back in the bag."

Sarah shuddered again.

"And those two other thugs carried me from Arphaxad's wagon to the other man's wagon. But instead of putting me into the back with the other bags, the two thugs put me up front on the floor of the wagon seat. I heard Arphaxad and the other man talk some more, then the other man continued driving south out of the City of Cain."

Elihu couldn't help but ask, "Was the other man the Captain Blackheart that Arphaxad told us about?"

"The one and the same. I was now a slave, sold at the slave market to Captain Blackheart, the most notorious slave trader in the world."

Sarah shuddered.

*   *   *   *

"Well, as all of you know," Crista continued, "I was never one to keep my mouth shut for long. After bumping along for awhile, I spoke to the driver: 'Who are you?'

The man did not respond.

Well, you know that I never took silence for an answer. So I asked him again, and his response was the same."

Adah wondered, "Did you ever get him to talk?"

"Of course," Crista answered. "I had much experience irritating my brother . . ."

"Amen to that!" Methuselah teased back.

". . . so I put on my most irritating feature, my voice. I started singing to him."

Sarah blurted out, "Singing!?!"

"Sure," she replied. "I started singing 'They that wait upon the Lord shall renew their strength.' I sang it through three times before the driver cracked."

Adah giggled. "What did he say?"

"Well," Crista chuckled, "he said, 'Young lady, I don't know who your Lord is, but I can assure you that you are not going to fly away, run away, or walk away. However,' he added, 'I would appreciate it if you would faint.'"

Adah giggled again. "At least he had a sense of humor."

Elihu was not amused.

Adah asked, "Did he ever say anything else?"

Crista went on with her story. "Not until I started singing again. Then he asked me, 'Young lady, what will it take to stop you from your infernal singing?'"

Elihu could not help but ask, "Why didn't he just slap you or kick you or something like that?"

"Ouch," she exclaimed. "I learned that evening that I was precious cargo. I told him that I would stop singing if he would let me out of the bag. Quick as a wink, he untied the bag and moved his sword off of his seat, placing it next to him on his right side. With some difficulty, I can tell you, I wiggled out of the bag, and in less than a ladylike fashion, I was soon sitting next to him."

Elihu gave Crista a stern look. "What exactly do you mean 'less than a ladylike fashion?'"

"What I mean," she explained, "is that you should try to sit up in a wagon seat while your hands and feet are tied, trying every moment to avoid a sharp sword that looks like it is itching for a fight. Anyways, the older crew member gave me a very stern look, much like Elihu just gave me, but it seemed at the time that they never questioned any of the decisions of Captain Blackheart. So, I sat there on the front seat, as far away from the driver and his sword as I could, carefully examining the countryside for any possible escape route.

After several miles, I felt compelled to break my silence. So I asked the driver the same question I had asked before: 'Who are you?'

He replied, 'Young lady, you are breaking your promise.'

Well, I was not going to let him impugn my honor. 'Sir,' I replied, 'if indeed Sir is an appropriate name for a slave trader such as yourself, I did not break my promise. I promised to not sing again.'

He looked over at me for the first time, then asked: 'What will it take to stop you from talking?'

I smiled and said, 'Probably an act of God.'

He smiled back. 'I don't know your god. I can't negotiate with him, only with you. What can I do to stop you from talking?'

'Untie my hands and feet,' I said.

'Keep talking,' he said. 'But you only get three questions.'

'Fine,' I said. 'Who are you?' I asked again.

'Captain Blackheart.'

'Never heard of you,' I countered. He just shook his head as I asked my second question.

'Where are we going?'

'The port city of Livernium, southeast of the City of Cain.'

I mulled that answer over in my mind. I had never been to a port city, but somehow, I had a feeling that I did not want to visit Livernium. While I was contemplating his answer, Captain Blackheart spoke up. 'You have one more question, young lady.'

I pondered for about two seconds what to ask, then said, 'What are you going to do with me there?'

He very calmly explained that he was going to put me and the other slaves on his ship, sail down south, and sell us to interested buyers.

'Whoa!' I thought to myself. I took a glance at the bags behind me and asked another question: 'Why are you treating me so special?'

Captain Blackheart quickly raised his right index finger and calmly said, 'Sorry. You have exceeded your limit of questions. No further talking.'

I was fine with that. I had heard enough. I needed time to think and to plan an escape. He noticed when I glanced down at his sword. His last words to me during that day's drive were, 'If you touch that sword, I'll have to kill you.'"

*   *   *   *

Methuselah spoke up. "Speaking of time, Crista's story is going to take forever to tell if all of us keep interrupting. Why don't we just hold our questions and comments until later. Crista, why don't you just tell your story like a good storyteller would?" Everyone agreed, and Crista continued with her story.

Chapter Eleven

On the Road
to Livernium

The journey to Livernium was dreadfully monotonous, mind and body numbing. Although we passed many travelers, no one seemed to pay much attention to a young lady sitting in the front seat of a wagon, with both her hands and feet tied. Apparently, slave trade had become common enough in the settlements southeast of the City of Cain.

We stopped that night along the road, just before the last rays of sun fled the sky. Any expectations of better treatment lasted for only a few minutes. The two younger crew members, ordered around by the mean looking older guy, started taking the bags out of the wagon and dumping them on the ground. When all of the other slaves were unceremoniously dumped on the ground, the older crew member walked over to my side of the front seat. He had a wicked smile on his face as he reached for me, when all of a sudden the sword of Captain Blackheart flashed before my nose.

The hands of the crew member stopped in midair. "First Mate Letch, you take care of the other cargo. I shall take personal responsibility for this young lady."

Let me tell you, First Mate Letch was none too happy that he didn't get to grab me. A snarl formed on his face, followed by, "Yessir, Captain Blackheart. Whatever you say, sir."

I didn't budge. That sword, only two inches from my nose, didn't budge either until Letch moved to the back of the wagon. Then I looked back and heard the first mate tell the two younger crew members to build a fire, then to fetch some fruit and water from the area. When they left looking for firewood, Letch started moving among the bags of human cargo, groping each one until he found what he wanted. Without a word, he lifted that bag over his shoulder and walked away from the camp. I didn't want to think about what happened, but he came back later, after everyone else had eaten, shoving the point of his knife into the back of a woman he had been with.

The slaves were always bound hand and foot, but allowed out of their bags long enough to eat and relieve themselves. Captain Blackheart ate alone in the wagon, feasting on a roasted animal that one of the younger crew had cooked over the fireplace. I ate with the other slaves, chomping slowly on a large apple pulled from a roadside tree. One of the other slaves was an older teenage girl named Rebekah. Like everyone else, her clothes and hair were rumpled from hours of riding in the large wagon. She ate her apple as if she were a starving animal. She had a wild look in her eyes. She told me that she had been a slave for five years, sold three times by Captain Blackheart, and now headed for her fourth owner. "All of them were old men who liked young girls, who used me until they tired of me." When I didn't eat my apple core, Rebekah asked me for it. I bargained with her. "First, tell me why I am receiving special treatment from Captain Blackheart." She grabbed the apple core, swallowed it in two bites, and explained, "Because you are fresh fruit, not spoiled."

I was sitting next to Rebekah when Letch and the other woman returned. Rebekah scrambled behind me, trying to hide from the first mate. She whispered in my ear, "You must stay away from him, Crista. He likes young girls, and he has never tired of me."

After dinner, Letch and the two crew members stuffed all of the slaves back in their bags and dumped them back in the wagon. Rebekah had told me earlier that it was easier for them to keep track of us at night that way. I watched with disgust as Letch made sure that he only handled female slaves. And then I watched in horror as he walked toward me, holding a bag.

Just as he was raising the bag to place over my head, the air whistled as a dagger landed between Letch's feet. We both looked up and saw Captain Blackheart calmly eating a leg of lamb, carving off slices with his sword. Letch snarled, but backed away.

Captain Blackheart spoke to me. "Young lady, bring me my dagger." Frankly, I wanted to grab it and stab Letch in the back, but I noticed that no one disobeyed the captain's orders. While bringing it back to the wagon, he calmly swished his sword in the air. As I nervously laid the dagger where I had sat earlier, the captain asked, "Young lady, would you care for the rest of my leg of lamb?"

I looked up at him dumbfounded. "Leg of lamb?" I mean, my Daddy was a shepherd. I could never eat one of those cuddly little lambs that we raised. "Sir," I replied, "it is a sin to eat lamb or any other meat."

The captain was amused. "Who says?"

"My Daddy says," I answered.

"I do not take orders from your father, whom I have never met."

"Well, the Tales of Father Adam tell us that we should not eat meat."

"Young lady, I do not take orders from Adam, whom I have never met either."

"Well," I sputtered, "it's really God Who told Adam in the Garden of Eden to not eat meat."

"I am sorry, but I have never met this god that you mention. I don't take orders from him, either."

I was speechless for several moments. The captain spoke again. "Good! I like to see you that way." When he finished eating, he took me down to the river to wash. Then we walked back to the wagon, where he retrieved his bed roll. He laid it out near the fire, then spread out another blanket near him. When he laid down and fluffed his pillow, I mustered the courage to ask him, "Aren't you going to put me back into my bag for the night?"

He closed his eyes and rolled over. "Silly girl," he answered with his back to me, "if you try to escape, Letch will find you." I pondered his words for a few moments, then laid down on the blanket near Captain Blackheart, and fell fast asleep, strangely comforted by being so near to the slave trader, my security blanket.

Day after day was the same. I stayed as close to Captain Blackheart and as far away from Letch as possible. With each new day, I met more and more slaves. Most of the women had numbed their minds and bodies to their daily fears and depravations at the hand of First Mate Letch. Only one or two were like Rebekah, a wild animal, still resisting the insults to her body and mind. I resolved, no matter what happened to me, that I would be like Rebekah.

*   *   *   *

Near the evening of the thirteenth day, we came over a hill, and there in front of me, far away, was the Great Sea. I never knew there was so much water in this world. An entire city spread out from the waterfront, and there were ships in the water, looking like model boats from that distance. Even then, I could see that some ships had sails, and some had oars, and some had both. I wondered which ship was Captain Blackheart's. As we rode down the hill, I caught the smell of the sea, a salty smell that was new to me. I don't know why, but for some reason, I liked the smell. The thought occurred to me: Maybe, when I make my escape, I could become a sailor.

As we neared the town, other smells assaulted my senses. I could smell, from dozens of ovens, the hateful odor of burning animal meat. And I could smell another odor, a strange odor I had never smelled before -- the odor of fish. I shook my head. Were people eating fish, too?

The City of Livernium was not walled in. There were houses scattered about, and a large marketplace, and a place I later came to know as the docks, where ships were tied to wooden walkways extending from the shore out into the water. Men were walking up and down the docks, carrying boxes and bags, hoisting them onto ships or taking them off. I was just as fascinated by the docks as I had been by the marketplace in the City of Gom. I wanted to run around and examine every ship; but of course, my hands and feet were tied. I would be able to examine only one ship on my first visit to Livernium.

Captain Blackheart drove the wagon toward one of the largest ships in the harbor. The ship had a name -- *Lucky Lady*. I didn't know if there was such a thing as luck, but if there was, I had been the lucky lady of the lot of slaves so far. The ship was a pure sailing vessel. I learned later that Captain Blackheart was so proud of his sailing skills that he did not believe he would ever need oars to help move his ship into and out of the docks. The ship had two masts, one fore and aft, each about thirty feet tall, with booms attached about eight feet above the deck. The sails were furled, laying atop booms, secured by rigging which rose from the boom to the top of each mast. No other ship in the harbor had dual masts. I didn't know it at the time, but I should have been impressed.

As we neared the ship, I noticed other features on the deck. There was a platform, aft of midship, where two huge oars nearly met, extending aft both port and starboard, into the water. The two oars were obviously too high to effectively row, so I wondered if they were some sort of steering mechanism for the ship.

I also noted a cabin aft of the platform, with windows all around and a door facing fore. I was not familiar with ships then, but I assumed that the cabin was for the captain. I did not see any other place for the crew or human cargo to berth. Later, I was to discover that the crew slept on deck and the slaves below deck in some dark, smelly holds. I also noted that a small rowboat, a little dinghy, was tied on to the starboard side; I assumed its purpose was for the crew to go ashore in some harbor where the large ship could not dock.

First Mate Letch shouted out, "Ahoy, mates!" to the crew members aboard ship. The crew made sure that the ship was securely cabled to the dock and that the gangplank was in place. The crew, supervised by Letch, started hauling bags into the ship. I watched with horror as a hatch was raised amidships, and the bags were carried down to the holds. I waited for my turn, wondering if my "luck" had run out.

As I sat there next to Captain Blackheart, Letch approached and asked with a gleam in his eye, "Captain, if it be your delight, I shall take the rest of the cargo down into the hold."

I trembled. The captain rose from his seat, stepped down onto the dock, and replied, "No, First Mate Letch, that would not be my delight." As the gleam faded from Letch's eye, the captain continued. "It is too late to set sail tonight. Arrange to have my horse stabled for the night and my things taken to the Shark's Teeth Inn." As he started to leave, he announced, "We set sail in the morning." As I sat there in the wagon, watching my protector walk away, leaving me alone on the dock, I saw the first mate leer in my direction. As terror rose up in my throat, Captain Blackheart looked back, snapped his fingers, and called out, "Come, Crista. Don't keep my dinner waiting."

Chapter Twelve

The Captain's Cabin

Captain Blackheart did not speak to me again that night. Still bound hand and foot, I shuffled behind him to the Shark's Teeth Inn, checked in with him, sat at his table during dinner, and slept on the floor in his room that night. In the morning, before daylight, he arose and wrapped a long, red sash around his waist. While we ate breakfast downstairs, one of his crew gathered his belongings. I followed him each step of the way as he walked to his ship, afraid to let him out of my sight.

The crew unfurled the sails as we boarded the *Lucky Lady*. The captain led me to his cabin, opened the door, and invited me in. Then he closed the door behind him and took out his dagger. I didn't know what to expect. I gritted my teeth and warned him not to touch me. He simply ignored me, knelt down and cut the bonds on my feet, then sliced open the bonds on my hands. I was startled. He calmly said, "I don't advise you to leave." Then he whirled and left his cabin.

I sat in the chair at his desk and rubbed my hands and ankles. Free at last, I thought. Then, I slumped my head on his desk and cried.

A few minutes later, I felt the ship moving. It was an exhilarating feeling, gliding through the water. I looked out the starboard window and saw the dock retreating. I ran to the fore window and watched the mouth of the harbor close in on us. And then, whoosh, we were out in open sea, the ship tacking one leg after another, faster than any horse could ever dream. We were flying!

Captain Blackheart did not return to the cabin until noon. He surprised me since I was looking out the starboard window, admiring the coastline off in the distance. "What are you looking at, young lady?" the captain asked.

"The big, blue sea, the graceful seagulls, and the distant coastline." I was nearly giddy.

The captain just shook his head. "Lunch will be served soon. Set that table."

I obeyed immediately. Looking over at the captain, intrigued by his outfit, I asked, "Why did you wear that red sash this morning?"

He looked down at the sash, wrapped several times around his waist, then tightened it. "My father taught me that a sailor should be ready for any eventuality. A sailor never knows when he may need extra cloth to tighten or patch a sail, or to lash cargo down, or to bandage a wound." He looked out the fore window. "Sailing can be a dangerous business."

I was more interested in food than danger. Flying across the sea gave me an appetite. Several minutes later, one of the crew members brought a leg of lamb, a loaf of bread, butter, bananas, apples, and honey. I ate everything, except the lamb, of course.

After we ate, the captain indulged in his normal habit of using a toothpick to clean between his teeth. Even aboard ship, he was, well, tidy. He stared across the table at me, a thing that he hardly ever did, and told me to stand up. Of course, I obeyed immediately. "Turn around," he ordered. So I turned around quickly. "No," he insisted, "slowly." After examining me thus, he said in a low voice, "You'll do."

Well, I wasn't quite sure what "You'll do" meant, but I was still just a child, only twelve years old. Then he looked at me right in the eye and asked, "Crista, do you know why I bought you from Arphaxad in the slave market?"

I stammered, "I-I-I think so, sir. I have talked to the other slave girls."

"Good," he replied. "I do not wish for you to think of me as your protector."

"Well," I quickly responded, "I am grateful that you have kept me out of the clutches of that evil Letch."

"Only because it suits my business purposes, young lady, not because I have any affection for you."

"No, of course not, sir," I retorted. "And I certainly have no affection for you."

He coughed. "I see you merely as a business proposition; nothing else has ever entered my mind."

"Of course not, sir, but I am grateful that you have treated me like a proper young lady, excepting of course for the bonds on my hands and feet."

He grumbled something to himself, then said, "You have plenty of spirit, young lady. From where I sit, that quality adds exceptional value to how much I can ask for you."

"Thank you, sir. My father and mother have always placed a high degree of value on me."

He grumbled again, then said, "I was told that your father was dead."

I looked right into his eyes and replied, "You better hope so, sir, if you value your life."

He pushed back from the table, stood up, and walked to a window. "You must have been quite difficult to live with back home."

"My brother would agree with you, sir."

He erupted, jerked around, and pointed his right index finger in my face. "Young lady, do not toy with me. I could have you tossed overboard, or worse, tossed to the crew."

I smiled. "Ahh, but you can't do that, sir. I am too valuable a business proposition."

He stormed to the door and glared back at me. "Miss Crista, I must admit that if you were a man, your feisty spirit could have made you a fine sailor. But now, I will be delighted when this journey is over and you are the responsibility of someone else who may be able to put a line around that feisty spirit of yours."

"Begging your pardon, sir, but my value to you in any future business propositions would be lessened if any man puts a line around my spirit. You don't want to tarnish your goods, do you?"

That was too much. He jerked open the door, glared back at me, and started to say something else, but stomped outside and shut the door behind him.

I rushed to the door to hear anything outside. I could hear the voice of the first mate, who apparently could hear much of the conversation in the captain's cabin from his roost on the platform. "Begging your pardon, Captain," he started, repeating the captain's words, "but I would be delighted to help you out by putting a line around that girl's spirit."

I could hear the captain spit. "Letch, if you come within ten feet of that young lady, I will have you tossed overboard to the sharks. That young lady is the prized cargo on board this ship."

"Yes, Captain. Whatever you say, Captain," I could hear him hiss. "That young lady is certainly a prize."

*   *   *   *

I spent the afternoon watching the distant shoreline and the beautiful seagulls. I overheard conversations outside, including a conversation between the captain and first mate about our destination. The captain sounded worried. "Letch, this whole trip has taken too much time. My buyers are anxious, especially the old man who wants the young girl. I can't tell you how hard it is now to find young girls like that who are still untouched." Well, let me tell you, I didn't know what side of the world the captain was from, but I knew quite a few girls back home who still valued their purity.

Letch came up with a scheme to improve the captain's business propositions. "Begging your pardon, Captain, but there is a shortcut."

Captain Blackheart took the bait. "What's that, Letch?"

"You see," Letch explained, "we are wasting our time hugging the coast. We could save two days time if we pointed our rudders west southwest, straight across the Great Sea."

By this time, figuring that both men were deep in the conversation, I poked my head above the window sill of the fore window to watch them. I saw Captain Blackheart shake his head. "It's much safer staying within sight of land," he insisted.

"Aye, Captain," Letch responded, "but remember what you often tell the crew? No risk, no reward. Now's the time to take a little risk."

The captain bowed his head, pondering the possibilities. Then he looked up and ordered, "Change course, First Mate. New heading, west southwest." Before he could execute the order, the captain warned him, "But don't stray too far south, Letch. Stay the course."

Letch exulted, "Aye, aye, Captain." Shoving to the left and turning the steering oars to the right, he shouted to the other crewman: "New heading. Changing course to west southwest." The ship responded immediately, and catching new wind, sped off on its new bearing. Before I ducked my head down, I caught an ominous gleam in Letch's eye.

Chapter Thirteen

Mutiny on the Lucky Lady

Captain Blackheart did not return to the cabin until the sun was almost below the horizon. He, along with all of the other sailors, enjoyed the thrill of speeding out to sea, even though the waters were not well charted. As long as the wind freshened and they kept their bearings, they hoped to make up valuable time on this journey.

When the cabin door finally opened that evening, I turned my head from the starboard window. "Sir," I questioned, "I have not been able to see the coastline or hear the seagulls for some hours."

"Of course not, Crista," he explained. "We are heading straight across the sea in order to make up time."

"Are there any dangers on the open sea?" I asked.

He took off his sword, dropped his dagger on the table, and remarked, "There are great white sharks in the Great Sea, but since they have not yet learned how to sail a ship, I think we have little to fear from them." Then he ordered me to set the table for dinner.

The captain was looking at some charts by candlelight when his dinner was delivered by the cook, an unkempt man who looked at me the way Letch did.

The captain sat down and started carving up a chunk of roasted beef and drinking a foul-smelling drink which he favored, a drink made from boiled leaves. "Aagghh," the captain spat while drinking what he called tea, "This new cook will be the death of me." I calmly sat and ate a slice of bread with butter spread over the top. The captain's mood worsened as the meal wore on. His eyes seemed to become unfocused for a minute. He stood up unsteadily and said he must go out for a breath of fresh air. As he turned toward the door, he stumbled to one knee, then fell over on his side.

I screamed, jumped up from the table, and ran to the door to call for help. As I opened the door, Letch and the cook stood staring at me from just a few feet away. On either side, all of the other crew members were spread out, each holding a spear or dagger in their hand. "Letch," I cried out, "Captain Blackheart has fallen ill."

His eyes gleamed at me. "'Tis a pity," he replied. "But he ain't the captain no more, young lady. I am."

I could not believe my ears. "Are you daft, man?" I screamed. "Your captain needs your help."

"Begging your pardon, little lady, but unless someone on board ship has an antidote for the poison he just drank, well, I'm afraid there's nothing any of us can do for him."

His words struck like a dagger in my heart. "You foul beast!" I snarled at him.

"Yes, little lady, that I am," he chuckled, "more foul than you know. But I do have a remedy for your ignorance, as you shall learn later this evening in the captain's cabin." Then he turned to the other men and ordered them to throw the captain overboard. "There are sharks in these here waters, you know."

I didn't know what would become of my life, but I could bargain for the captain's life. "Stop! All of you! First Mate Letch, let me make a bargain with you."

Letch held up his hand to stop the other men. "That'll be Captain Letch to you, young vixen. What's your bargain?"

"Captain Letch," I said, "let me give my life for Captain Blackheart's."

He shook his head. "What are you talking about, little lass? That poison will kill the captain, I mean the former captain, in less than an hour."

"If you are so certain," I replied, "then place his body in the dinghy and set him adrift without any oars."

"And why should I do that?" he demanded.

"Because," I said, "if anyone conducts an inquiry into what happened to Captain Blackheart, then you and your men can truthfully say that it appeared that he abandoned ship during the night."

Letch leaned over and consulted with the cook for a few moments, then said, "Supposing I agree to do that, little lady, what do I get in return?"

"One moment," I said as I briefly retreated a few steps into the cabin. When I returned to the door, my right hand was behind my back. "If you place the captain's body in that dinghy," I bargained, whipping my right hand from behind my back, flashing the captain's dagger in front of me, "then I won't take my own life."

Letch stepped back at that threat. "Don't be hasty, little lady. Don't be hasty." He consulted with the cook, then responded to my new offer. "Seeing as how there ain't no ships or islands in this part of the Great Sea, I guess I could accept your generous offer." He ordered a couple of men to prepare the dinghy. "Now you take care of yourself real good while a couple of my men come in and drag Blackheart out." I backed away, out of reach of the men, as they entered the cabin and dragged the captain's limp body out onto the deck. I followed them to the door to make sure the captain's body was deposited in the dinghy. As I reached the door, a hand lunged for the dagger. Without thinking, I slashed the knife toward the hand, sending blood flying everywhere and sending a sailor screaming across the deck.

Letch backed away even further as I threatened to stab myself. "Come look for yourself, you little vixen." The crew backed away as I slowly walked out of the cabin, holding the dagger near my stomach. I walked to the starboard side and saw the captain's body lying crumpled in the dinghy. "Now, sweetie," Letch said, "you keep your end of the bargain." As he took a step toward me, I raised the dagger above my head, screamed like a wild animal, and thrust down with the dagger. Of course, I missed my stomach completely. Instead, I used that moment of confusion to take a running leap toward the dinghy. As I leaped in, I cut one of the lines holding the rowboat to the ship. As the dinghy started tilting, I grabbed for the captain's body to keep him from falling out, and Letch reached over the rail and grabbed for me. As he grabbed my left arm, trying to pull me back up, I reached over, slashed his arm, then cut the other line, sending me, Captain Blackheart, and the dinghy toward the water. Letch screamed and tried to let go of me in time, but the sudden drop of the dinghy caused him to lose his balance.

There was a huge splash in the water as the dinghy hit on its side. I landed on Captain Blackheart's stomach, which cushioned my fall, but I felt the dinghy starting to capsize. Just then, Letch's back hit the topside of the dinghy, causing the dinghy to right itself in the water. As he slid off the side of the dinghy, Letch inadvertently shoved the dinghy further away from the ship.

It was pitch black down in the water. I heard Letch cry out, "I'll get you, you little vixen. You'll pay for this." But he didn't know where the dinghy was. He was thrashing around, trying to find us, screaming to the men on board to get some light over the side. Suddenly, I heard him screaming again: "Help! Help!" I felt a thump under the dinghy, and then Letch screamed again: "Shark! Shark! Help me!" The shark must have been attracted by the thrashing in the water or by the scent of blood, or both. There was more thrashing, more splashing, and more screaming, and then the night grew quiet. The dinghy drifted west away from the ship, which turned its bearing to the north.

I lay down in the dinghy to catch my breath. I wasn't hurt, save for some bruises where Letch had grabbed me. I felt around for the captain's dagger, which I dropped when the dinghy hit the water, but I couldn't find it. Then I knelt down to listen if the captain was still breathing. When I did, I smelled a foul odor. I reached down near his mouth and felt a wet, lumpy substance. Ugh! He either had a wave of nausea, or the pressure of my landing on his stomach caused him to lose some of his dinner. As I backed away from the vomit, my hands felt another wet substance. I held a little to my nose. Blood!

I checked all over my body for wounds. I couldn't find any. Then I checked over Captain Blackheart's body, starting with his head. His left temple was crushed. He must have hit the dinghy hard when the rowboat hit the water; but there wasn't any blood. I felt his chest and back, and still couldn't find any wounds. After taking a deep breath, I started feeling around his lower body. Just behind his right knee, I found the wound . . . and the dagger. Blood was gushing out of the wound like a fountain. When I grasped the handle of the dagger, I heard the captain groan. He's still alive, I thought. But when I pulled out the dagger, the fountain spurted even higher. "He's going to bleed to death," I cried.

I clumsily took off his sash, ripped off a strip, and tied it tightly around the thigh. I prayed that the fountain would stop flowing, and it did. I ripped off some more of the sash and tied it around the wound. I put my ear up to the captain's mouth and heard his shallow breathing. My heavy breathing had to slow down, so I sat down in the dinghy. I looked around at the vast blackness, only seeing a few stars shining dimly overhead and, off in the distance, a receding, shimmering light in the direction where the *Lucky Lady* had sailed away.

* * * *

I took some deep breaths and considered my situation. I was in a dinghy with no oars, in the middle of a shark infested sea, far from any islands or shipping lanes, with an unconscious man who had been poisoned, had a concussion, and had nearly bled to death, with no food and no water. I quickly concluded that I would rather be in the dinghy than aboard ship.

Chapter Fourteen

Home Was a Dinghy

I had never prayed very much as a child. Prayer was something that Daddy did before meals and sacrifices. I had seen Momma pray many times, but I never gave it much thought. I mean, how much could a housewife pray for?

Much. Very much. My first prayer, after waking up in the early morning darkness, was that my Momma was praying for me. She had connections with God.

I didn't know about my Daddy. If he was alive, I knew that he would come looking for me. But I didn't know if he was alive. The last time I had seen him, his crumpled body, with his head caved in, lay limp in the marketplace of Gom. I prayed for my Daddy.

And I prayed for the man in the dinghy with me, a man who reminded me a little of my father -- crumpled body, head caved in. Yep, that man needed prayer.

I didn't really know how to pray, or where my prayers went, or if my prayers were heard. I just knew that it felt good in my soul to ask God for help. Then I fell asleep.

*   *   *   *

Many hours later, when the sun was high in the sky, I was greeted by blood and stomach upheaval smeared all over the captain and the dinghy. This cannot do, I thought. So I unwrapped the tourniquet, reached over, and started wiping up the mess. When the sash became too saturated, I leaned over the boat to rinse it out in the sea water.

My hand flew back in the dinghy. "What am I thinking?" I scolded myself. Just in time, my memory clicked in of Letch flailing in the water, blood oozing from the cut in his arm, blood that was sending out signals to nearby sharks that dinner was being served.

Where else could I dispose of the blood and vomit? I didn't want to be sitting in this dinghy staring at that stuff all day long.

I didn't want to be in the dinghy at all. I wanted to be home, waking up in my bed, safe, looking out the window at the orchard, smelling biscuits in the oven. I wanted to be home.

Now, home was a dinghy.

*   *   *   *

I did my best to clean up the dinghy and the captain. All of the mess I could clean up ended up in the bottom of the boat, winking up at me from time to time during the day.

I was amazed that the captain was still breathing. That poison was supposed to kill him. But it hadn't, yet. Maybe God, wherever He was, had heard my prayers.

Then I had another thought. Maybe death by poisoning would be preferable to how we were going to die out here in the middle of nowhere. The captain had lost a lot of blood, more than I ever wanted to see again; and much of his remaining blood had pooled in the deep purple bruise spread across the whole left side of his face, where he bumped his head the night before. I wouldn't want to go through life with a misshapen head like that. Who knows what trauma his brain had suffered.

But the real danger was from the knife wound. It was still oozing a little bit of blood from the bandage. I used the dagger to cut his pants leg off above the knee, then stripped the bandage off, taking more skin than I could imagine. At least the captain's groans sent me a signal that he was still among the living.

But when I looked at the wound under the bandage, I nearly fainted. The captain wouldn't want me to faint now, I thought. So I leaned over to the middle of the dinghy and added my vomit to the captain's.

"What am I going to do with that?" I wondered. There was blood and pus oozing from the wound, which was larger than I had imagined. I knew I had to clean it up somehow. Looking down at the sash, I knew what I had to do next. I tore off another large section of that sash, and with more courage than I thought I ever had, I dipped it into the sea water, praying that no sharks were nearby. When my hand surfaced safely, I started wiping away the blood and pus from the wound. I did my best, but I wished then that I had paid more attention when Momma had cleaned my wounds when I was a child.

When I was a child!?! I thought. I was still a child, only twelve years old. Somehow, life didn't seem very fair at the moment.

The wound was very red, very deep, and the scarlet lines of infection were spreading. Where was

Momma's herb garden when I needed it? I cried to myself. I sat back in the boat, closed my eyes, tilted my head upward, and prayed to a merciful God that He would perform the impossible -- raise up Momma's herb garden in the middle of the sea.

I sat there for a few moments, my eyes closed to the glaring sun, at least enjoying the swaying of the dinghy in the deep blue sea, when all of a sudden, I could feel the swaying slowing down. My immediate wishful thought was that maybe we had landed ashore. But from where I sat, all I could see was blue sky all around. So carefully, I opened my eyes and looked overboard.

Green stuff. Lots of green stuff, sea weeds or something, surrounded the dinghy, keeping it steady, keeping us from moving very fast, keeping us stuck out here in the middle of the sea. "Oh, God," I cried, "please get us out of here!" Once again, my mind went back to Daddy's homestead. How I wished I could be back there. I would never again complain about doing chores around the house. I would never even complain about pulling weeds from Momma's herb garden.

Weeds! Herb garden! I looked over the side of the dinghy and laughed at the sea weeds, the large floating herb garden which God raised up for me. Maybe I didn't know where God was, but now I had proof that He knew where I was, and that He heard my prayers.

I fearlessly reached over the side of the boat and grabbed up gobs and gobs of sea weeds. I didn't care that it was wet and slimy. I just rejoiced and laughed as I wiped the captain's wound with the green stuff. After the wound was as clean as I could get it, I packed some sea weeds around the cut and the infected areas. Then I tore off some more of the sash to make another bandage, and wrapped it loosely around the sea-weeded wound. When I was done, I reached over and grabbed more sea weeds for the next time that I changed the wound. I then leaned back in my seat, spread my arms, let out a deep breath, and smiled. "Thank You, God," I said to the heavens. But then I had another thought. I was still in the dinghy.

*   *   *   *

By the time that the sun went down, the large, floating herb garden was long gone, my skin was burnt, and my throat was parched. I was tempted to drink some sea water, but somewhere in my mind I seemed to remember someone saying that sea water was for fish, not people. I was also tempted to chew on the sea weeds, but I wasn't sure if I should eat anything saturated with sea water; besides, most of the sea weeds had slipped down into the bottom of the filthy dinghy.

At least the captain was still breathing, though still unconscious. Would he ever wake up? I asked myself more than once. I made myself as comfortable as possible and fell into a peaceful sleep filled with dreams of home.

*   *   *   *

My peaceful sleep was rudely interrupted an hour before sunrise by a furious shaking. Fear of capsizing alternated with hope of rescue as I peered uselessly into the utter blackness. Then I heard a groan and realized that Captain Blackheart was having convulsions, threatening to send himself or me or both overboard. As carefully as I could, I went to his side and felt his forehead, which was burning with fever. I didn't know what to do. How could I calm him down and lower his body temperature? I was frantic. The furious rocking of the dinghy was sure to attract the sharks.

I almost fell overboard. Sea water splashed in the boat. Without thinking, I caught myself, cupped a handful of sea water, and threw it where I thought the captain's face would be. Furiously, over and over, I splashed water on his face and body while his convulsions constantly threatened to toss me overboard. I touched his forehead again, but he was still too hot. Until the sun came up, the captain kept convulsing and I kept splashing his face and body.

As the first rays of light spread across the sky, I briefly examined the mess that our dinghy was in. Sea weeds were mingled with blood and vomit, the water level on board had lowered the dinghy dangerously close to the water line, and the captain's eyes were rolling around in his head during his incessant convulsions. I checked his forehead, and at least his raging fever had subsided. And then I realized that the lower the dinghy was in the water, the less it swayed with the captain's convulsions.

Then, his thrashings became even more furious. I nearly fell overboard again, then the captain nearly fell overboard. "Lord," I cried, "help me."

At that moment, I was thrown toward the captain's side of the dinghy. Landing on top of the captain's body, I rode out his convulsion. As his arms and legs continued to thrash, I pressed down hard upon his body on the boat. "Don't tip us over, Captain Blackheart!" I cried. I held on to him tightly, wrapping one arm under his seat and the other arm on the side of the dinghy, waging a fierce battle with my fears and the captain's body. The battle went on and on and on until my muscles ached all over. I knew I could not hold him down much longer.

And then, when my strength gave out, his next convulsion tossed me overboard. Only my right hand held on to the edge of the dinghy. With my body swaying to and fro with the rocking of the boat, I desperately prayed that the sharks weren't around and that I could get my left hand on the side of the boat and pull myself up.

Just then, I felt something brush against my leg. I looked over and saw a shark fin floating away from me. Suddenly, it turned and headed straight for me. Frozen with fear, I thought, This is it. Before I could will my body to move, the captain had another convulsion which almost tipped the dinghy on top of me. As I reached up to protect myself, I grabbed the front of my seat with my left hand. Then the dinghy tilted the other direction, and the upper half of my body slammed into the boat. As I scrambled to get my feet in, the shark rammed the side of the dinghy.

I went sprawling into the captain's body. I saw a second shark circling on the other side of the dinghy; before I could set my feet, the second shark rammed the boat from the captain's side, almost knocking me back in the water. As I caught myself, my right hand brushed against the captain's dagger. As the first shark came in for the kill on my side, I planted my feet and waited. His huge nose and mouth lunged toward me, and I drove the dagger down hard on his snout.

As the shark flopped back, the dinghy scooted away from him, causing me to lose my grip on the dagger. The last I ever saw of that dagger was seeing it embedded in the shark's snout, sending blood gushing forth, spreading across the water. Then I saw the other shark circle the boat again, smelling the blood, opening his jaws wide, going for the blood. There was much thrashing and splashing in the water, and the dinghy floated further and further away.

Chapter Fifteen

Our Last Day at Sea

I must have fallen asleep. I was dreaming that someone was softly calling my name, "Crista, Crista." Then I heard the gentle voice again. "Crista, Crista." I opened my eyes, and there, right in my face, were the green and gray eyes of Captain Blackheart staring up at me. "Crista, Crista," he softly said, "what in the world are you doing lying on top of me?"

I was so startled that I nearly rolled off the boat. As I corrected myself, I rolled toward the center of the dinghy, splashing in the mixture of blood, vomit, sea water, and sea weeds. I quickly scrambled into my seat on the other side of the boat as the captain tried to sit up. He didn't make it. He grabbed his leg, then grabbed his head, plopped down on his seat, and groaned. "Please," he said, "would someone please stop the throbbing in my leg and the pounding inside my skull."

I looked over at him. The only brilliant conversation I could think of was, "You're awake."

He groaned again. "If this is awake, let me go back to sleep." As he closed his eyes again, I actually was quiet for a few minutes.

I could tell from the captain's movements that he was not successful in going back to sleep. After a few minutes, he spoke up while lying in his seat. "Crista, speak to me."

I laughed. "Now, that's a new request, Captain Blackheart."

The captain chuckled, then groaned. "Don't make me laugh, young lady. It hurts too much." With his eyes closed, he began to talk some more. "Does my head look as bad as it feels?"

I was honest with him. "Worse."

He moaned again. "I assume that we are no longer in my ship's cabin."

"Safe assumption, Captain."

"And I assume," he continued, "that we are no longer aboard the *Lucky Lady*."

"Right again, Captain."

"I must tell you, young lady, that I am not very fond of your answers."

"Me neither," I replied.

He mumbled something, then asked, "So where are we?"

"Don't have a clue, Captain," I answered. "Floating adrift somewhere out in the middle of the Great Sea."

The captain groaned. "Dreadful! Just dreadful!" he exclaimed. "I never should have let the first mate talk me into taking that shortcut." Then he asked, "How did we get here?"

"We floated," I replied.

The captain almost laughed. "I had nearly forgotten how irritating you can be. Now, tell me what happened."

So I did. I told him how Letch and the new cook plotted to poison the captain's tea. "Blasted first mate! I should have gotten rid of him long ago." Then I told him how Letch ordered his men to throw the captain overboard and how I bargained for the captain's life. "That was quite decent of you, young lady," he said with some appreciation. Then I explained how Letch never intended to lower the dinghy, but that I used the captain's dagger to slash the lines. "Do you still have that dagger, Crista?" he asked. "I would very much like to slash Letch's throat with it some day."

"Begging your pardon," I replied, "but I don't think you'll be doing that." So I explained how our dinghy came crashing into the water, which explained the bruise on his left temple, and how Letch fell overboard with us. "I had slashed and bloodied Letch's arm with your dagger, which probably explains why the shark showed up."

"Shark!?!" the captain exclaimed.

"Don't worry, Captain. The shark didn't attack us then . . ."

"Then!?!"

"I'm coming to that," I said. "Anyway, First Mate Letch won't be causing you any more trouble, sir."

The captain could not believe his ears. "I am astounded that the other crew members did not come to our rescue. That is the Code of the Sea."

"Begging your pardon, again, sir, but all of those crew members were mutineers."

The captain shook his head and looked over at me. "What is this world coming to?"

I stared back at him. "Well, if you could ask my Daddy, he would probably say that the world came to meat eating, and then slavery, and then who knows what other wicked thing the world will come up with next."

The captain glared. "I am not fond of your impertinence, young lady. You should treat the captain with more respect."

"Begging your pardon, sir," I firmly stated, "but I've never heard of someone being the captain of a dinghy."

"Hmmpphhh!" he mumbled. He closed his eyes, then reluctantly continued. "I suppose I should thank you for saving my life." Without actually thanking me, he then ordered me to tell him about the other wound, the sharp pain in his leg.

"Well, actually, sir," I answered, "your leg valiantly protected your dagger from falling into the sea when the dinghy crashed down from the ship."

The captain grunted. "Very noble of my leg. How much blood did I lose?"

"Fountains," I answered. Then I explained how I did my best to clean up his wound after I threw up in the dinghy.

The captain smiled. "I am sorry that I was such a bother. But you know, it was a good thing that you heaved in the dinghy, not overboard. Sharks can catch that scent, also."

I just nodded my head as he asked me about the sharks. I told him that I would describe the shark attack, but that first I wanted to tell him about the sea weeds. So I described how I was dreaming and praying about my mother's herb garden, when all of a sudden our dinghy was surrounded by a floating herb garden. "Do you believe in prayer, Captain Blackheart?" I asked.

"Young lady, I believe in the sun god and the moon god and the sea god and any other god that makes people feel good, but I don't believe in a god who answers prayer." Then he quizzed me. "Do you?"

"Well," I honestly answered, "I have never thought much about God, although my family was religious. I guess if there was a God when I was growing up, I didn't have much need for Him." I paused, then said, "But, I confess, I have thought more about God the last couple of days."

"I hope it makes you feel better," the captain commented. "Now, tell me about the sharks." So I told him how he was having convulsions, and the boat was rocking wildly in the water, attracting the sharks. I explained how I was thrown overboard and then thrown back aboard just before the first shark rammed the dinghy.

"The first shark!?!" Captain Blackheart shrieked.

"Yes, sir." I continued to explain how I was nearly knocked over the other side of the dinghy, and then the second shark rammed that side. "As I flew to the other side of the boat, my hand found the dagger. When the first shark reached his jaws up into the boat, I rammed the dagger into his snout." I described how the first shark slid back into the water, with the captain's dagger firmly implanted in his snout, and how the second shark followed the scent of blood and attacked the first shark.

The captain was quiet for a few moments. "Young lady, I'm afraid that I am in your debt more than once for saving my life."

I shook my head. "Ahh, Captain Blackheart, you would have done the same thing."

He shook his head. "I'm not so sure, young lady. I'm not so sure."

*   *   *   *

He lay quietly for quite awhile. I thought he had gone back to sleep, but then he spoke up. "Crista, you said that the cook had poisoned my tea, is that right?"

"Yes, Captain," I replied.

"I remember," he continued, "that the tea did not taste very good. At first, I just chalked it up to the poor galley skills of the new cook. But it was more than that, wasn't it?"

"Yes, sir," I replied. "First Mate Letch claimed that the poison would kill you within an hour."

"But it didn't, did it?"

"No, sir."

"Even though I was badly bruised on the head and badly wounded in the leg. I should be dead, you know."

"I'm glad you're not, sir."

"Very decent of you to say so, young lady." He pondered my answers, then continued. "And you told me earlier that I lost fountains of blood from my leg wound, right?"

"Right, Captain."

"Hmmm," he paused. "That doesn't explain it all. Perhaps some of the poison left my system through my wound, but I am certain that Letch and the cook would have placed enough poison in my tea to kill a horse. At least, it tasted that poorly."

As I thought back to that night, the captain asked me another question. "Crista, you mentioned that you heaved while cleaning my wound the first time." Then he carefully asked his final question: "Was there a time that night, when I was bruised and wounded, that I lost some of the contents of my stomach?"

I remembered falling from the ship's side, into the dinghy below, cushioning my fall on the captain's stomach. "Begging your pardon, sir, but you made quite a mess in the bottom of the dinghy."

When I explained that to him, he exclaimed, "That's it! That's why I did not die from the poison. Much of the poison ended up in the bottom of the dinghy." He paused, folded his hands together, and closed his eyes again. "I'm afraid that you have developed quite a nasty habit of saving my life, young lady."

I looked over at him. "Kind of strange, isn't it? Almost providential."

He turned his head and looked over at me. "I don't know this god that you speak about, Crista, but if he truly does exist, I might like to meet him someday."

I nodded my head. "Me, too, Captain. Me, too."

*   *   *   *

The captain fell asleep, and I did, too. When I awoke, in the late afternoon, Captain Blackheart was sitting up. "Good afternoon, Crista," he said cheerily.

I rubbed my eyes and asked, "What was that?"

The captain was quizzical. "What was what, young lady?"

I stretched my arms wide, yawned, and replied, "There was a certain pleasantness in your voice. I didn't know that you had any."

He laughed. "Young lady, you have a remarkable talent for irritating people."

I laughed in return. "Thank you, sir, and especially thank my brother Methuselah. He helped me to develop this talent to a keen edge."

"I should like to meet your brother some day," he mused.

I leaned back in my seat. "And I think my brother should very much like to meet the man who purchased his sister as a slave."

"Come, come," the captain exclaimed. "We must let bygones be bygones. After all that we have been through together, and after you have saved my life these three or four times, I could no longer sell you as a slave. I hereby release you from bondage. You are a free woman again, Crista."

I giggled, much to his consternation. Then I asked, "Free to do what?"

He nodded, then chuckled, then roared with laughter. "Crista, I hereby declare you to be the first mate of this fine sea-going vessel. Now, First Mate Crista, you are free to die as a sailor."

I saluted him and said half in jest: "Aye, aye, Captain. Do you want me to go below to the galley," pointing to the mess in the bottom of the dinghy, "and prepare our last supper?"

"I would like that very much, First Mate Crista," he replied, with a renewed serious tone, "but I'm afraid that our food stuffs have been poisoned."

"How long," I asked, "can we survive out here without food or water?"

The captain thought for a moment. "Well, First Mate Crista," he replied even more seriously, "a healthy, full grown man could survive another two or three days perhaps." Looking around our little dinghy, he finished his answer. "But seeing as how we don't have any such sailors on board, I figure that we might last another day, maybe two at the most."

I pondered his answer for several minutes. Then the captain laid back down on his seat, closed his eyes, and said, "First Mate Crista, it seems that *Lucky Lady* has deserted us." He sighed deeply, then uttered his last words of the day. "Before you go to sleep tonight, I would appreciate it if you would say your prayers."

Chapter Sixteen

Landfall

I awoke with a start. There seemed to be more stars than usual overhead. Something was different. I could feel that the captain was shuddering in the cold of night, maybe even having some more convulsions; but they were not nearly as violent as before.

As I lay there, I realized that the dinghy was moving more rapidly. The current is stronger, I thought. And that's when I first noticed it. A different sound. That's what was different. I sat up quickly and jutted my head forward. Yes, off in the distance was a new sound that I could not place. At first, it just sounded like a hum, like geese flapping their wings overhead. I jostled the captain and told him to get up. He rolled over with a moan and a grumble. "Captain," I said again, "you must get up. I hear something unusual."

He ignored me. I didn't know what to do, so I kicked him in the back. He jerked up and warned me, "I'll have you flogged for that, sailor." I ignored his threat and whispered, "Listen. I hear a sound."

The captain rolled his head around, rubbed his eyes, listened for a moment, and said, "I don't hear anything. Go back to sleep."

I couldn't believe it. I felt like kicking him out of the dinghy to wake him up, but decided on another course of action. I cupped my hand and splashed water

on the captain's head until he finally sat up. The sound
was getting louder, and the captain could finally hear it.
A look of surprise spread across his face as he exclaimed,
"Breakers!"

"Breakers!?!" I replied with a hopeful heart. "Is
that like land?"

"Yes," growled Captain Blackheart, "but not
the kind of land we want to meet." We both looked
forward and could make out something faintly white in
the distance. "Crista, the current is taking us straight
toward those rocks."

"Rocks!?!" I cried.

"If this current carries us into the breakers," the
captain explained, "the dinghy could be smashed to
pieces on the rocks."

"What can we do, Captain?"

"Nothing, except stay low and hold on to the
dinghy as long as we can." He showed me the best way
to hold on. He laid flat on his stomach, facing forward,
and wrapped his arms around the bottom of his seat.
"Crista," he said, "if we stay low, maybe the waves won't
knock us out of the boat, and maybe the dinghy will skip
through to shore between the breakers."

He could tell that I was terrified, my eyes fixated
foward, the sound of crashing waves growing louder and
louder. The captain moved off of his seat and splashed
through the dinghy to my side. He grasped my head
between his hands and shouted, "You must get down,
Crista." He then started forcing my head forward,
and I finally stopped resisting him. As I laid down, he
reached over and wrapped my arms around my seat. As
the sound of the pounding surf grew louder and louder,

he shouted in my ear: "Stay down, stay in the dinghy!" Then he smiled, kissed me on the cheek, and promised, "I won't leave you or forsake you, Crista."

He stumbled back to his side of the dinghy as the boat started tossing back and forth in the steepening waves. Up and down we went, like a violent wagon ride, rising up in the air, then smashing down into the water, over and over again, waves coming over the side, filling my eyes, ears and even my mouth with water. The little dinghy was swamped with water, and I knew that we were soon going to sink. The captain yelled to me to hold on, and then the bottom of the boat scraped along a rock, the first land we had touched in several days, and maybe the last.

The little dinghy kept hurtling toward shore. I dared to look up as a huge wave lifted us higher than ever before, hoping it would toss us over the reef onto the beach. But as we came down, the dinghy smashed into a large rock sticking out of the water, exploding into matchsticks. My body slammed into the rock, losing my breath and any hope I had left. I tried to hold on to the rock, but I kept losing my grip, sliding lower and lower into the water below.

Just then, I felt something brush against my leg. I screamed, imagining a shark devouring me piece by piece on the reef. But then I felt a hand, then another hand, shoving my body upward. As I rose slowly above the water, I found one handhold, then another. When half of my body was lying on the rock, I held tightly to the rock with my left hand and reached behind me with my right. I felt around for the captain's head, but could only reach his hair, still submerged under the waves. I frantically grasped for his right hand, which suddenly went slack, and slipped away from me.

"Don't leave me now!" I cried. I thrashed wildly behind me and found his wrist. I held on and started to climb higher on the rock. I had to get his head out of the water. "Climb, Crista, climb!" I kept saying to myself.

Every second was agony as the waves pounded my back and threatened to loosen my grip on both the rock and the captain. Inch by inch, I crawled higher and higher. I looked back and could see the captain's hair. I kept climbing. I could see his forehead. I kept climbing. I could finally see his nose. I kept climbing. I could finally see his mouth. As he sputtered in the waves, he yelled to me, "Let me go, Crista!"

"NO!" I screamed back at him. "Hold on!"

He struggled to loosen my grip on his right hand. "Let me go, Crista," he cried. "Save yourself."

"NO!" I screamed again, inching higher on the rock.

He kept struggling to free himself. He shouted, "Crista, I think my back is broken. I can't make it. Let me go."

"NO!" I screamed back at him and glared into his eyes. "Climb, sailor, climb!" As I inched higher, Captain Blackheart swung his left hand upon the rock, but it slipped off.

"CLIMB, SAILOR, CLIMB!" I yelled. He flung his left arm upon the rock again and found a hold. As he inched himself upward, I did the same. Then a huge wave flattened us against the rock. I lost my grip on his right hand as his head went under water. I felt him fading away. I reached down wildly for his left hand, and found it still clinging to the rock.

I grasped his left hand and yanked his head above the water. "Don't let go!" I yelled. I climbed with my right hand now, and pulled him up with my left. Inch by inch, we climbed that rock together.

When I finally reached the top, I used both hands to pull him up. He was in shock, convulsing atop the rock, in danger of floundering himself off. Broken back or not, I could not lose him that way. I crawled on top of him, searched for handholds on the rock, and then did what I could to protect him from the waves and to give him any body heat that I had left. I lay in that position for hours, holding on, holding on, holding on, until fatigue swept my wakefulness away.

*   *   *   *

When I awoke, the first hint of morning rose from the eastern sky. I was still on the rock, and so was Captain Blackheart. The waves had calmed down from their nighttime fury. Indeed, the sea was nearly smooth, the waves gently breaking against the rocks. Although I was bruised and battered and sore all over, we were safe for the moment. I turned to the shore and blinked. It was only about one hundred yards away. There was no sandy beach, only a few rocks with trees beyond. I looked to the left and right, and I saw a beach about half a mile away on my right. The plan was simple. We would swim to the nearby rocks, then walk through the trees to the beach. Nothing could be easier.

As I rolled off the captain, he groaned. Thank God, he's alive, I thought. I looked around for any sharks and didn't see any. I touched the captain's face and spoke to him. "Captain Blackheart, we made it."

He opened his eyes. Neither his green eye nor his gray eye had much light in them. He forced a smile, then said, "Crista, you look terrible."

My vanity was not wounded. If I looked as bad as the captain did, with the left side of his face black and blue and bashed in from his earlier fall in the dinghy, and the right side of his face badly scratched and bruised from battling the rock last night, and his hands looking worse than his face, then I did indeed look terrible. Before I could rip off some clever banter, the captain groaned and closed his eyes again.

This was not the time for more sleep. I nudged the captain and told him that he and I should go for a pleasant morning swim. With eyes closed, he smiled again and said, "You go on without me, young lady. I'll just stay here for awhile."

I was not to be denied. I grabbed his shoulders to lift him up, when all of a sudden, he cried out in agonizing pain. I gently lowered him down to the rock. He grimaced and said, "Perhaps you should not do that again."

"Where does it hurt?" I asked, as quietly as I could.

He grinned ruefully and answered, "Everywhere but my legs."

*   *   *   *

Well, that was a starting point. As I reached to grab his legs, he stopped me with his right hand. "Crista, wait. You don't understand."

I looked down at him, frustrated by his hesitation. "What don't I understand, Captain?"

He exhaled deeply and replied, "Crista, my legs don't hurt because I can't feel them."

Chapter Seventeen

On the Beach

My hand flew to my throat and I gasped. My simple plan lay in shambles. "What are we going to do, Captain?" I asked frantically.

He continued to grimace. "We are going to do nothing," he answered. "You are going to swim to shore."

I was startled. "What do you mean? I can't leave you here."

Captain Blackheart sighed as pain wracked his body. "Somehow, I knew you would say that, Crista. But we must be practical. I would be no good as a ship captain without my legs. In fact, I am no good as a man without them." As pain enveloped him again, he pleaded with me, "It is best for all just to leave me here. If I don't have my sea legs, I don't want to live at all."

I laughed in his face. "Begging your pardon, Captain, but this is not the time for melodramatics."

He was indignant. "Now listen here, First Mate Crista. I order you to swim to shore and leave me here."

I smiled gently at him, looked around, and replied: "Captain, I don't see the *Lucky Lady* around here, and I don't see our dinghy either. Since you don't need a first mate anymore, I hereby resign. Prepare to swim ashore, sir."

The captain tried to spit at me, but it was too painful. "You are the most irritating person I have ever met."

"Thank you, Captain," I replied as I sat a few feet away from him, looking out at the gently breaking waves, wondering at the miracle of last night's survival. "Captain, do you remember the last words you told me before we hit the reef?"

He gruffly answered, "Remind me."

"You leaned over, kissed me on the cheek, and promised, 'I won't leave you or forsake you, Crista.' Do you remember that, Captain?"

"I'd rather not."

"And do you remember when we hit this rock, and I started to slip beneath the waves, that a couple of hands appeared out of nowhere to help push me up the rock?"

Captain Blackheart grunted. "Those were probably the hands of your god."

I smiled. "No, Captain Blackheart, maybe the hands of God gave you the desire and strength to save my life, but no, Captain, those hands were your hands, weren't they?"

He grunted again. "Have I told you lately how irritating you can be?"

I smiled again. "Well, Captain Blackheart, listen to me good." I got as near to his face as I could. "I won't leave you or forsake you, Captain Blackheart." Then I sat down and faced the shore.

The captain was quiet for several minutes. Finally, he coughed and said, "Crista, you should have let me go last night. And you should let me go today.

So I can't thank you for saving my life again. But," he emphasized, "I do want to thank you for one thing. Thank you for not kissing me on the cheek."

*   *   *   *

Captain Blackheart was not very cooperative as I grabbed him under the shoulders and dragged him down the rock to the water below. I wish I could have been more gentle, because he complained every moment on our way down; but I really didn't know any other way to do it. Once I eased his body into the water, both the pain and the complaining lessened considerably. Halfway to shore, he threatened to thrash around in the water until I let him go; I threatened to drown him if he tried a stunt like that.

The next stage of my brilliant plan was more difficult. I had to drag the captain's body over the rocks to the trees lining the shore. The captain didn't like that very much, and frankly, my strength was about gone when I finally laid him beneath a tree. We both lay there exhausted.

After a few minutes, the captain asked me what the next part of my brilliant plan was. So I told him that I had spotted a beach about a half mile away. He looked as indignant as someone racked with pain could look. "Are you going to drag me half a mile through the trees? Do you know how humiliating this is?"

I peered around in all directions. "Begging your pardon, Captain, but I don't see anyone staring at us."

"Well," he said, "allow me to make a suggestion." Then he described a very sensible plan to make sort of a cot with tree limbs, so he could lie flat when I dragged him instead of lugging him around under his shoulders. "Plus," he added, "I can sleep on the cot under the shade of one of those trees surrounding the beach, reminiscing about the days when I was something better than a beached whale."

I took my time to make the cot, and within an hour, we were on our way through the woods. The captain wasn't any lighter pulling him that way, and by the time we reached the edge of the beach, I was exhausted again. I was ready for a nap, but the captain asked me to turn the cot around so he could admire the view of the beach and the sea. As I slowly turned him around, a look of horror spread over his face. "I know this place," he whispered. As I looked down into his eyes, he cried out, "Flee, Crista, flee!" Then he passed out.

*   *   *   *

I was afraid to take my eyes off of the captain, hoping that he would say something else to warn me about this latest danger. But he didn't say anything. When he didn't even open his eyes, I swiveled my eyes from left to right. I didn't see anything dangerous, so I stood up straight and looked all the way around me. What was he warning me about? I screamed inside. I thought of sea monsters and wild animals. I thought of a thug hideout, with Arphaxad or Letch charging toward me out of the trees. "What danger!?!" I screamed out loud to an unconscious man.

*　　*　　*　　*

After a few more moments of hysteria, I started to giggle. It was funny. I mean, flee where? And if I had somewhere to flee, I couldn't very well flee fleetly with Captain Blackheart lying on a cot. So I decided to make the captain as comfortable as possible. I made sure his cot was as flat as possible and that he was as flat as possible on his cot. I was concerned about the sun burning his eyes and face during the day, so I looked around at the nearby trees and bushes, soon eyeing a broad leaf which I laid over his face. Then, I went on a quest for fresh water.

This place, whether mainland or island, was a paradise. I found a stream, bubbling with cool water flowing from a distant hill. I drank my fill, then thought about how to take fresh water back to the captain. I wandered around the stream, looking for anything that could hold water, when I spotted a fallen tree. Some of its bark was lying on the ground, so I took some of it and molded it into something that, from a distance, might look like a cup. Then I tore some fresh branches off of a nearby bush and wrapped them around my makeshift cup to hold the pieces of bark together.

I rushed over to the stream to try out my new cup. I scooped up some water and started running back toward the beach. I had not taken ten steps before all of the water leaked out. So I stopped and wondered what to do next. As I wandered along the bank of the stream, praying to God for help, I stepped in a mud puddle.

I don't know why, but I moved back to that fallen tree and started to cry. After all of the perils we had gone through, stepping in a mud puddle was insignificant. But I looked down at my shoe, caked in mud, and just wept my eyes out. After a few minutes of feeling sorry for myself, a very simple thought occurred to me. I walked back to my favorite mud puddle, scooped up some mud, and started lining the inside of my beleaguered cup, squeezing and draining as much moisture as I could while forming the mud to conform to the shape of the bark. After just a couple of minutes, the inside of my cup was fairly smooth. I walked back to my tree and placed the cup on a sunny part of the trunk. Then I sat down with my back to the tree, closed my eyes, and fell right to sleep.

I don't know how long I slept, but when I got up and checked my cup, the mud had hardened. I scooped up some water from the stream and held the cup up. Ten seconds. Twenty seconds. Thirty seconds. A minute. No water drained out. I raised my cup in victory.

Within a few minutes, I was forcing the captain's mouth open and pouring drops of fresh water down his throat. Then I went back and got another cup of water. That went on for about an hour. The sun was already past noon.

*   *   *   *

Now, my stomach growled. Spotting several orange trees across the stream, I waded over, reached up, pulled down an orange, and then fell to my knees and prayed. "Oh God, I don't know where You are, but I thank You that You know where I am. Thank You for protecting me and Captain Blackheart. Heal him, O

God, and guide both of us to You. Amen!" That done, I tore open the orange, peeled off a section, and placed the juicy orange in my mouth. I hadn't eaten anything that tasted so good for days.

After eating the orange, I picked several more, carrying them in my upfolded skirt. I walked back to the beach, hoping that the captain was awake, but he was still asleep. Good for him, I thought, as I stored the oranges at the base of one of the trees. I looked at the tree, wondering what it was. I don't think I had ever seen that type of tree before, but as my brother knew, I rarely noticed things like that back home. Back home! Would I ever see home again? Or would this place become my final home?

"Well," I said to myself, "if this place is going to be my home, I may as well make it into a home." So I thought about a house. Then I realized that I didn't have the first clue about how to build a house. I mean, I thought I had accomplished a major building project when I built a cup. "The captain may be in more trouble than he knows," I chuckled to myself. So I decided to wait until the captain woke up. Surely he would know more than I did about how to build a house.

And then I had another thought. A house? I didn't want to live in the same house as Captain Blackheart! We would have to build two houses.

*   *   *   *

That afternoon, I made several more trips to the stream, trying to keep myself and the captain hydrated. As the sun was going down, it began to get chilly, so my thoughts turned to building a fire. I was sure I could do it. I mean, Methuselah had once told me how I could rub two sticks together to make a spark that could ignite some leaves.

After gathering some leaves and sticks, I was feeling pretty handy as I started rubbing two sticks together over a pile of leaves in the sand near where the captain was sleeping. After about thirty minutes, when the sun was almost down, I got my first spark. After another ten minutes, I was able to ignite the leaves. As I proudly watched the leaves burn, they almost burned out. Frantically, I tossed my two sticks on top of the leaves and groped around for some more wood. After another ten minutes, with a roaring fire going, I knew I was ready to burn up the world.

In the light of the fire, I took the broad leaf off of the captain's face and squeezed some orange juice on the captain's lips. When is he ever going to wake up? I thought to myself more than once in the gathering gloom of night. What were those dangers he warned me of? Could I fight them off alone? As I replaced the broad leaf on the captain's face, I had a selfish thought: Why did you have to pass out?

*   *   *   *

Sometime later, enjoying the warmth of the fire, I had another thought. Maybe a passing ship would see my fire on the beach. Maybe we would be rescued that night or in the morning. But then I had another thought. Maybe the dangers that the captain had warned me of would be on that passing ship. Or maybe the danger was on this island, or wherever we were, and my fire was sending a smoke signal, or a smell signal, to some land shark or other wild beast. Or maybe my imagination was running wild. I decided to just relax, enjoy the warmth and another orange, and let the dangers come what may. I ate an orange, added some more logs to the fire, and curled up near the fire for a good night's rest.

* * * *

I don't think I was asleep for very long when I heard a strange noise. I jerked up, looked over at the fire, and saw a log shifting. "Get a hold of yourself, girl," I told myself. "You're too jittery." So I laid back down, closed my eyes, and heard that noise again. I lay there frightened to death. Something was lurking in the woods. A land shark? A wild beast? Arphaxad? Letch? All sorts of visions reared their ugly face in my head. Then I heard two noises. Oh, no! I cried to myself. There's more than one monster.

* * * *

I finally worked up enough courage to slowly open my eyes. I saw the gleam of two red eyes in the trees behind the captain. And then I saw two more eyes several feet away from the first. I knew just what to do. I crawled in the sand over to the captain and whispered, "Wake up, Captain. Wake up." But he didn't. He kept sleeping. I jostled his back and said more loudly, "Wake up, Captain." But he still didn't.

I was prepared to obey the captain's last command: "Flee, Crista, flee!" My feet were ready to jump up, run down the beach, and dive into the water. But in my heart, I knew I could not desert the captain. If we were going to die, we were going to die together. Scared half to death, I leaped up and screamed into the night, "Come on. Show yourself. I'm not afraid of you!"

I wish I had not been so foolishly bold. I suddenly saw two spear points emerge from the darkness. As the weapons advanced, I saw who was holding them -- hideous looking creatures, creatures with scabby faces, creatures wrapped in layers of filthy cloths. One of the creatures had no nose. The other one didn't have all of his fingers on his left hand. "Oh God, protect us!" I cried out loud.

Chapter Eighteen

The Island of Hideous Creatures

As I stood there speechless, with my heart in my throat, the mouth of the creature on the left, the one with missing fingers, opened. "Good evening, young lady," a pleasant voice spoke. "We mean you no harm."

What trick was this? "Who are you?" I screamed. "Why are you threatening us with spears?"

The speaker immediately dropped his spear, as did the creature on the right. The speaker extended his arms palms outward, in the universal sign of someone without a weapon. "Sometimes visitors to our island are not as harmless as you appear to be."

Island? I thought. Great! Captain Blackheart and I are marooned on the Island of Hideous Creatures. As the speaker stepped forward, I challenged him. "Don't come any closer! Who are you?"

The speaker stopped suddenly, bowed, and said in a gentle voice, "My name is Mandrake." Then he introduced his younger companion as Javan. Mandrake spoke again. "We mean you no harm, young lady, but it appears that you and your father are injured."

I snapped a quick glance at the captain, his head still covered by the broad leaf, and blurted out, "I'm feeling fine, and he's not my father."

Mandrake lowered his head and eyed me suspiciously. "Is it common in your country for a young lady to travel with a man not her father?"

I let out a deep sigh and lowered my internal defenses. "Mandrake," I answered, lowering my arms, "it's a long story."

"I'm sure we will have time to hear it," he replied. He reached into a bag on his hip and pulled out and put on thin gloves on his hands. "In the meantime, do you mind if I conduct a physical examination of your, uhh, er, uhh, friend?"

I threw my hands up in the air. "Sure. You first might want to know that he has been poisoned, had his head smashed, suffered a severe knife wound behind his right knee, and most recently, I think, broke his back when we shipwrecked."

Mandrake lowered his eyes, smiled slightly, and asked, "Is that all?"

I began to chuckle, and so did Mandrake. I felt an urgent need to correct one matter. "Actually, Mandrake, it wasn't exactly a shipwreck. It was more of a dinghywreck."

For the first time, Mandrake betrayed some emotion, as his voice rose: "You were out in the middle of the Great Sea in a dinghy!?!"

"Like I said earlier, it's a long story." As he neared the cot, I spoke again. "My name is Crista, and this man here is . . ."

"Yes," Mandrake interrupted as he knelt by the cot and removed the broad leaf from the captain's face, "I have met Captain Blackheart before." I watched as he carefully examined the huge bruise on the left side of the captain's head. Mandrake softly spoke to Javan: "Severe bruising, fractured cheek bone, left temporal fracture, and almost certain concussion." Then he slightly lifted the captain's right leg, causing the captain to moan, while Mandrake carefully unwrapped my bandage and peeled away the remaining sea weeds. Feeling around the knife wound, he calmly reported to his companion: "Deep puncture wound through the muscle and ligaments, almost to the kneecap. Adequate field dressing to reduce infection, but in need of immediate cleansing and rebandaging."

I was fascinated by the examination. Mandrake lowered the captain's leg, then rapped just below his right knee sharply with his knuckles. Again, in that soothing voice, he told Javan: "No reaction. His spine is either severely bruised, with significant swelling, or worse, broken." He turned to me and asked: "Crista, did you apply the field dressing on his right leg?"

I wasn't sure what I had done wrong, but I truthfully answered. He promptly responded: "You certainly saved Captain Blackheart's leg, if not his life." Then he examined the cot that the captain was lying on. "Did you make this cot?" he asked.

"Yes, sir," I replied, "according to the captain's instructions."

"Ahh," sighed Mandrake deeply. "So the captain has been conscious since suffering his concussion."

"Yes, sir. We have been through quite a bit the last several days."

He stood up, took off his gloves, threw them in the fire, and gently told me. "Captain Blackheart may live if he receives immediate medical attention. But sad to say, Crista, he may never walk again."

I don't know why, but tears formed in my eyes. Mandrake averted his eyes for a few moments before asking me kindly: "Are the two of you close?"

I lowered my head, and sighed. "Mandrake," I answered, "perhaps it would be best to say that Captain Blackheart and I have had a short, somewhat combative relationship."

He stood there, nodding his head, and said, "Sounds familiar."

*   *   *   *

Mandrake whispered something to Javan, who then dashed off into the trees. I was startled. "Where's he going?"

"Back to the village, Crista."

"Aren't you two going to carry Captain Blackheart there for medical treatment?"

Mandrake looked down at his patient, then looked up into my eyes. "Crista," he started, "the captain should not be moved. His back . . . ," he trailed off.

"Oh," I exclaimed, feeling rather stupid.

"And besides, Crista," Mandrake continued, "I am certain that Captain Blackheart would not want to be carried to the village."

In the firelight, I tried to read Mandrake's face. "How could you possibly know that?" I asked.

He slowly turned and walked slowly through the sand toward the water's edge, motioning for me to follow. I hesitated, but then figured I didn't have much to lose. As he stopped and looked out into the black-ness of the night, listening to the gentle lapping of the waves upon the beach, I walked over and stood near him. After a few moments, still looking far off into the sea, he softly said, "Crista, you are kinder than most strangers are when they first meet people like Javan and me."

I focused in my mind how insulting I was to them when I first saw them, so I tried to imagine how I could have been more irritating. But then, in my mind's eye, I focused on my first thoughts when I saw them: the Island of Hideous Creatures.   "Well," I said, "my Momma and Daddy always taught my brother and me to be kind to strangers . . ." I didn't finish the rest of that sentence: ". . . even if they don't have fingers and noses."

Mandrake read my mind, even finishing my sentence for me, chuckling and asking, ". . . Even if they don't have fingers and noses?"

I looked over at my host, seeing only the vaguest features of his face in the distant glow of the firelight. "You have a kind face, Mandrake, not like Javan's."

He thought for several moments about my comment. "I have not always had a kind face, Crista. For most of my life, I had a proud, haughty look about me." Then he turned to stare at me. "But one day, my face will turn unkind again, like Javan's face."

"What's wrong with Javan's face?" I innocently asked. "What happened to his nose?"

Mandrake held up his left hand, which was missing the two fingers next to his pinkie finger. "Don't you understand yet, Crista?" he explained. "You and Captain Blackheart are marooned on Leper Island."

Chapter Nineteen

The Tale of Captain Blackheart

Mandrake was such a nice man, I didn't want him to see the terror that was spreading from my heart to my face. As I turned away from him, I thought again of the horror that morning on Captain Blackheart's face and his last words to me: "Flee, Crista, flee!"

No disease on Earth was more dreaded than leprosy, slowly destroying flesh and nerves. No people on Earth were more despised, social outcasts doomed to live life alone or with other lepers, forced to cry out "Unclean! Unclean!" whenever a "Clean" person inadvertently approached.

My mind returned to my thoughts earlier that morning, and I started to giggle as I turned my face back toward Mandrake. A look of surprise crossed his face, and with a quizzical voice he said, "Most people such as yourself would not find being marooned on Leper Island a humorous situation."

"Think about it, Mandrake," I replied. "Captain Blackheart and I are so badly bruised and battered that if we walked into your village, the others would probably not notice that we are not lepers."

"That is true," he admitted.

"In fact," I continued, "why don't you hereby anoint the captain and me as honorary lepers?"

"You have a most unusual sense of humor, young lady."

"I blame it on my older brother Methuselah," I retorted.

"I am not sure that I want to meet him," Mandrake chuckled.

I waved my arms and pointed them out to sea. "Look, Mandrake, when Captain Blackheart recognized this beach earlier this morning, he cried out in horror, 'Flee, Crista, flee!' But we had no place to flee to. And besides, I told the captain that I wouldn't leave him or forsake him."

"Admirable notion," Mandrake replied.

"I wasn't ready for Leper Island, Mandrake, but you should be concerned for the welfare of the others here. Is Leper Island ready for me?"

*   *   *   *

The captain moaned very loudly then, and I dashed back to the cot to see if he had started a new round of convulsions, but he hadn't. That reminded me to explain that medical condition to Mandrake, who appreciated the new information. "I can see that you care for the captain, Crista, another unusual aspect of your personality. For his health's sake, why don't you describe your relationship with the captain. It will be another couple of hours before Javan returns, so take your time."

For the next twenty or thirty minutes, as we sat around the fire, Mandrake listened intently as I recounted my adventures of the last month. When I reached the point in my story about being placed in the captain's cabin aboard the *Lucky Lady*, Mandrake nodded. "Ah, yes, the *Lucky Lady*. Crista, allow me to ask a delicate question. At any time before or during your journey on the *Lucky Lady*, did the captain ever mishandle you or approach you in an inappropriate manner?"

Of course, I had thought about that matter more than once. I explained how the captain treated me as a mere business transaction and protected me merely to protect his investment in unblemished goods. Mandrake mulled over that answer, then asked: "Did you notice that Captain Blackheart is more cultured than your typical captain?"

"Begging your pardon, sir," I answered. "I wouldn't know. I have never met any other captains." I paused, then finished answering: "But the captain is certainly more cultured than First Mate Letch."

"Ah, Letch the Lech. Is that reprobate still carrying on with the women?"

Dreadful memories surfaced, causing my voice to crack. "I don't believe so, sir. He's dead."

"Justice is done," he sighed. "Blessed be the name of the Lord."

I was startled when Mandrake used the name of the Lord. "Mandrake," I blurted, "do you know the Lord?"

"Why do you ask, Crista?" he wondered.

Then I explained how God seemed to protect both Captain Blackheart and me during our incredible journey. "Remarkable," Mandrake murmured. "Do you know the Lord, Crista?"

I had to answer honestly. "No, sir." I then briefly told him about my father's retelling of the Tales of Father Adam, but how my father's faith seemed to be so sterile, nothing but vain ritual. "Crista," Mandrake said soothingly, "your father sounds like he was a good man who didn't really know the Lord."

"You seem to know the Lord, Mandrake. Where did you meet Him?"

He smiled. "I first met the Lord right here on Leper Island."

"Here!?!" I gulped. "The Lord lives here, on Leper Island!?!"

He nodded his head and pointed to the stars above. "Not as His official dwelling place," he explained, and then pointing to his chest, "but here in my heart. And I continue to meet with Him every day."

"Do you think that maybe I could also meet God here on Leper Island?" I asked hopefully.

Mandrake stared at me. "Young lady, you seem to care for those who have protected you these last few weeks. I should very much like to introduce you to the Lord, but first, would you mind if I told you more about your human protector, Captain Blackheart?" I told Mandrake that I would be delighted, so I settled in the sand and listened to the tale of Captain Blackheart.

* * * *

Blackheart was the son of a rough and tumble captain from Livernium and his wife Lilith, another one of Cain's high priestesses married off to an ambitious young man eager to make his mark in the world. The elder Blackheart was selected by Cain to help develop a new business, slave trading. After a couple of years of marriage, Lilith accidentally became pregnant. As was Cain's practice, eight days after the baby girl was born, Lilith presented her firstborn to Cain as a sacrifice to the Great Ebony Cow.

The elder Blackheart, outraged at the needless and heartless death of his daughter, took his anger out on his helpless wife and helpless slaves, becoming a wife beater and slave beater of the worst sort. Only the loss of business income from maltreated slaves caused the elder Blackheart to reduce slave abuse, leading him to expend his rage more exclusively upon his wife.

That's when Lilith became pregnant again. She threatened to kill her baby in the womb unless her husband stopped beating her. Only then did the elder Blackheart's rage subside and a semblance of peace return to their small home in Livernium. The slave trading business thrived, and the captain had a bigger house built in Livernium.

The baby was born, a healthy boy with one peculiar feature -- his right eye was green, and his left eye was gray. The captain loved his son and spent as much time as possible with him when he came home from his slave trading trips. However, Lilith was an inattentive mother, only interested in lounging around the new house, letting a maid brush her hair. When the boy was five, while her husband was on one particularly long business trip, Lilith had one of the upstairs rooms decorated with garish crimson walls, white woolen carpeting, bright chandeliers, and an ebony cow along one wall.

Upon return from the sea, her husband was furious at his wife's initiative. When he threatened to tear out all of the new furnishings, Lilith explained that such a room, which she called a worship center, was part of his contract with Cain. The captain went berserk, taking his sword and hacking the walls and the chandeliers and the dumb ebony cow, forbidding his wife to ever allow such things to enter their home again.

One month later, after another business trip, the captain returned home to find his wife sitting in their bedroom, her hair being stroked by the maid. Lilith calmly stood up, hugged her husband, and told him that she had a surprise. She led him down the hall to the room formerly used as a worship center. When she opened the door, everything was back to how it had been before -- crimson walls, white carpet, chandeliers, and the dumb ebony cow. The captain backhanded his wife, drew his sword, and stormed into the room.

But also inside the room was a squad of priestly guards, led by a man called Chief Priest Theron, who told the captain to put away his sword. Instead, the captain swung his sword, and would have lopped off Theron's head, except for the parrying movement of one of the guards. The other guards quickly tackled the captain and held him on the ground. When Theron leaned over to slap the captain in the face, the captain spit in the chief priest's face.

After being roughed up by the guards, the captain was plopped at the feet of Theron, who was sitting in the chair underneath the ebony cow. Theron kicked the captain, spat in his face, and explained the facts of life to him: Lilith's worship center was going to be used to expand the cult of the Great Ebony Cow and raise support for a new temple in the Livernium market-place. The captain could either get on board or forfeit his profitable slave trading business. And then Theron left with one final warning: Don't abuse Lilith's face or body, both of which would be necessary for the growth of the worship center.

That afternoon, the captain packed up some things for his son and moved him aboard his ship, the *Lucky Lady*. He refused to allow his son to live in such a home; and Lilith didn't mind losing such a distrac-tion to the growth of her worship center. But after one short trip, the captain realized that a five-year-old boy was too young to live aboard a slave trader. When he returned home, the captain made arrangements to take a trip with his son to the City of Cain.

*　　*　　*　　*

As Mandrake was telling me the tale of Captain Blackheart, he suddenly became teary eyed. He paused, wiped his cheeks, and said, "This is where my wife and I enter the tale."

I blurted out, "You have a wife?"

"Yes, Crista," he answered. "My wife Naamah and I had been married at that time for about ten years. I was an associate teacher at the School of Humanism, under the leadership of that great intellect, Lamech-Cain. I needed some extra income, and my wife and I had been wondering if we would ever have any children of our own. That's when the captain came to the city looking for someone to board and tutor his five-year-old son. My wife took one look at that green and gray eyed little boy and leaped at the opportunity, so we kept the young boy at our home for the next five years. Naamah taught the boy discipline and proper manners during the day, and I handled his academic topics during the evening."

Hmmm, I thought. That explanation helped to explain why Captain Blackheart was so well spoken and tidy. Mandrake wiped another tear from his eye and added, "Naamah and I came to love that boy. One of the saddest days of our life was when the boy was age ten, and his father made one of his frequent trips to the City of Cain. I'll never forget his words: 'The boy's had enough schooling. Now he needs to learn to be a man.'"

Then Mandrake described how the captain took his son on board the *Lucky Lady* as the cabin boy, teaching him everything he knew about ships, sailing, and the slave trade. The lad was an apt pupil, becoming the spitting image of his father, a capable sailor at age twelve and an excellent first mate at age eighteen.

From time to time, between trading trips, the younger Blackheart re-developed a relationship with his mother Lilith, who had succeeded in building and dedicating a new temple in Livernium. By the time her son was twenty, his mother had younger ladies serving as priestesses, and she had more time to talk with her son. Those visits also helped to mellow the captain's rage over his wife's chosen occupation, and the family was even able to occasionally sit in the common room of their home and eat a meal together.

Everything was going smoothly for the captain and his son. The young man was looking forward to becoming a slave trader on his own someday. But

then an event occurred which has had consequences
to this day -- Lilith developed a sore on her left arm.
She treated it for several months, and naturally kept it
hidden from her customers. But the sore never healed,
and eventually another sore appeared on her right leg.
She managed the worship center for a couple of more
months, though of course not serving any customers
herself.

The turning point occurred when a sore appeared
on her left cheek. That she could not hide, so she retired
to her bedroom, attended only by her maid. When her
son came home from the sea, he discovered his mother's
condition.

The younger Blackheart recoiled. In his many
travels, he had seen many lepers, hideous creatures
wrapped in cloths, with blood and pus oozing from open
sores on hands, feet, arms, legs, and face. He knew what
was going to become of his mother. He struggled with
his emotions -- both natural affection and natural revulsion. He cried to his mother that she was a leper and that
she was going to lose everything she had built.

As she broke down in tears, the son called to his
father, who was eating downstairs. When the captain
came to his wife's bedroom, he was appalled. He, too,
recoiled from his weeping wife, then fell down on his
knees and began to sob. His son backed away from him,
too, never before seeing his father cry. Then the captain
began moaning that he had brought this curse upon his
wife and family. He grabbed his son's leg and cried that
he had been too greedy, that he had helped bring the
curse of slavery into the world, and that now God was
cursing him and his family.

*   *   *   *

As I was listening to the tale, wondering how Mandrake could know so much detail of Captain Blackheart's family life, I saw a light slowly coming down the trail which led to the village. It was Javan, holding a torch, with a bag of some sort on one hip and a jug on the other. Following him was an older woman, limping, her face ravaged by leprosy, carrying a bundle upon her back. Mandrake turned and called out, "Ahh, Javan, you have returned. Put your bag near the captain, and then get some fresh water from the stream."

As Javan walked back into the woods, I wondered if the old woman was a nurse. She walked straight to the prone body of Captain Blackheart, laid down her bundle, bent down, and looked carefully at the captain's face. Then, in a coarse, guttural voice, she exclaimed, "What a beautiful boy!"

Her comment seemed so out of place. What could be beautiful about a distorted, mangled, badly bruised visage? After staring at the captain for several more moments, the old leper woman stood and walked toward Mandrake and me. "Let me introduce you to Captain Blackheart's friend," he told the old woman. As she neared me, I noticed that her lips were gone. Mandrake joked, "She would shake your hand, Crista, but, you know, under the circumstances . . ." He trailed off. Then he made the introduction. "Crista, allow me to introduce you to Lilith."

Chapter Twenty

The Lord Taketh Away

I was never very good at hiding my emotions. I gasped. The deformed leper lady bowed, opened her lipless mouth, and uttered, "Thank you for taking care of my son."

I wasn't sure what to say, so I just mumbled, "It is a pleasure to meet you, Lilith."

She smiled, as much as a lipless person could smile, and simply responded, "Perhaps."

As I shifted from one foot to another uncomfortably, Mandrake interrupted the awkward silence. "Well, I'm glad you two ladies have met." Then he briefly explained to me that Lilith had not seen her son for twenty years, since the time that he dropped her off at Leper Island. He felt that it was only right to allow her this opportunity to see her son one final time.

"One final time?" I blurted out. "Are you telling me that the captain is going to die?"

"Perhaps," he uttered. "Whether he lives or dies, though, his mother will honor his wishes."

I shook my head. "I don't understand."

"It's a long story," he replied.

Then Mandrake motioned to me to kneel by the captain, and as he reached into the bag, he told me to carefully observe. Then he pulled out a jar, popped the lid, and laid the jar next to my hand.

I looked down at a jar of green goop, up at Mandrake's eyes, back down at the jar, then back up at Mandrake. "What's this?" I shrugged.

"Ointment," he answered. "Please apply it to the captain's face and hands."

Ointment!?! I thought to myself. Momma used ointment on us kids, and Daddy used another kind of ointment on the sheep, but I had never applied ointment to anything or anybody. So I shrugged again and said, "I don't know how to apply ointment." Then I asked, "Why don't you do it?"

"Ahh, that is a good question, Crista." Mandrake explained that he was confident that the captain would prefer for me to apply the ointment and that I would do an admirable job if I followed his instructions. "Since you are hesitant, Crista, why don't you practice applying the ointment on your own bruised face and hands. You look hideous," he laughed, "like a leper."

His sweet humor was contagious. Both Lilith and I chuckled as I reached my right hand into the jar and scooped up a handful of green goop. Mandrake stopped me and told me that I should not apply so much at one time. I returned most of the ointment, and then started daubing my hands and face. The green goop was cool and refreshing, lifting my spirits. After finishing with my face, I held my hands on either side, adopted a serious pose, and sarcastically remarked, "Black and blue . . . and green. Do you think me . . . beautiful?"

* * * *

Under Mandrake's direction, I applied the green goop to the captain's face, which was burning up with fever. While I was applying the ointment, Mandrake explained the nature and extent of the captain's injuries to Lilith, who groaned more than once when Mandrake explained that the left temporal fracture was a probable contributing cause to the captain's convulsions aboard the dinghy and on the rock. Then Mandrake tried to lift Lilith's spirits by explaining that the captain might not suffer permanent brain damage since he had conversed in a clear and intelligent manner to Crista both during their dinghy cruise and after they had shipwrecked on the island.

Then Mandrake told me to apply the ointment to the captain's hands. "Crista," he cautioned, "you must be very careful as you move his hands. Any sudden or extreme movement could cause the captain considerable pain and perhaps worsen his spinal injuries." I was as careful as I could be, but every time the captain moaned, Lilith moaned, too.

Mandrake commended me on being such a good nurse, then told me that we would have to work on the captain's knife wound next. He scratched his cheek and talked out loud. "Hmmm. How are we going to lift his leg so I can get to the wound, without causing massive trauma to his back?" Just then, Javan returned with the jug of water. "Mandrake," I said, "all this nursing stuff is making me thirsty." So we took a minute for me to pour some water on my goopy hands, wipe my hands on my filthy skirt, then drink some water from a new cup that Lilith produced from her bundle.

While Mandrake was pondering and I was sipping, I had an idea. "Mandrake, why don't you and Javan lift up the captain's cot, and then I'll crawl under on my back and apply the green goop?"

Mandrake thought it was a splendid idea, except for one thing. Mandrake had to examine the wound, and I was far too small to hold up my end of the cot. Lilith solved that problem. "I never did much for my boy when he was a child, but I can help him now." So Javan grabbed one end of the cot, and Lilith and I grabbed the other end. Using all our strength, we lifted the dead weight of the captain's body, and Mandrake immediately crawled underneath the cot.

"Problem, folks," Mandrake said from underneath the cot. "I can't get to the wound. A couple of the branches are in the way." Before anyone could do anything, Lilith told me to grab both sides of our end of the cot. I obeyed without thinking and almost dropped the captain off the cot. The captain groaned, but I held on, and in a few seconds, Lilith dropped a knife into Mandrake's waiting hand. Then Lilith took her end of the cot before my strength gave out.

I could hear Mandrake whittling away at a branch, trying not to make too much motion. "Faster," I cried after a minute. "I'm about to drop my end of the cot." Lilith also cried out that she couldn't hold on much longer.

Mandrake dropped the knife, crawled out from under the cot, dashed to our end, and grabbed the cot just before Lilith collapsed in the sand. "Lilith!" I cried, kneeling at her side. She was breathing very heavily, but looked up at me, smiled, and said, "Take care of my son."

Without even thinking, I knelt over, kissed her forehead, and said, "I will."

Then I knelt down, crawled under the cot, and started whittling. Slowly, the branches gave way until I could see the wound. I spent more minutes making the hole larger so Mandrake could see how far the infection may have spread. Then I crawled out and told Mandrake it was his turn. He turned back to Lilith to ask if she could help carry the load now, but then his mouth stopped. Her eyes were staring into the sky, and she wasn't breathing.

"Lilith!" I cried, kneeling beside her body. Mandrake and Javan lowered the captain's body and rushed to the old woman's side. Mandrake pushed me aside and then straddled Lilith's body on his knees. He placed the palm of his right hand just below Lilith's breastbone, placed his left hand on top of his right, and pressed down firmly three times. Then he leaned over and placed his left ear next to her nose. Then he rose up and repeated that procedure three times. Then he pounded his fists together, rolled off the lifeless body, and started crying in the sand.

I leaned over to look at Lilith, and then I started crying, too. Javan stood over us, his head bowed, and uttered, "The Lord giveth, and the Lord taketh away. Blessed be the name of the Lord."

Without thinking, I moved over and placed that poor lady's head in my lap. I started to stroke her hair, getting stray pieces off of her face, wondering why God would take her at such a time as this. And then I remembered the last thing she told me.

I shifted, laid Lilith's head gently on the sand, and then stood up. "Get up, Mandrake!" I ordered.

Both men were startled at my command. Frankly, I was, too. I wasn't thinking. I was just reacting. Mandrake rolled over, knelt at the side of the still body of the old woman on the beach, and bitterly condemned his actions: "She was too weak. I never should have permitted her to help carry the load."

"Get up!" I ordered again.

Javan spoke up. "For pity's sake, Crista, give him a few minutes to mourn."

I whirled on Javan. "Listen up, you two. That woman carried Captain Blackheart for nine months at the beginning of his life, and it was a privilege for her to carry him again at the end of her life." Then I knelt down, jerked up Mandrake's head, and yelled at him. "The last thing Lilith told me was to take care of her son, and the last thing I told her was that I will. Now, are you two going to help me take care of the captain, or are you going to just wail and whine like a couple of old women?"

Mandrake looked up at me, tears pouring down his face. "You're right," he whispered, trying to stifle a smile. "I don't know if Leper Island is ready for Crista."

Chapter Twenty-one

The Tale of Captain Blackheart and Mandrake

The procedure was simple. I knelt on my hands and knees on the sand next to the cot, the two men lifted the cot, placing one end on my back. Then Mandrake let go of his end, crawled under the cot, and examined the wound. In a carefully modulated voice, he said, "The infection is the source of his fever, spreading rapidly. He may lose his leg."

I felt like all the breath was pushed out of me. I silently cried out, "O Lilith, I'm so sorry. I'm not doing a good job of taking care of your son."

Mandrake crawled out from under the captain, reached into the bundle, and produced another jar. He opened the lid and placed the jar under my nose. It stank to high heaven, a foul red liquid which made me gag to look at and sniff it. "Crista," Mandrake implored me, "in just a minute, you and I are going to change positions." Then he explained how he was going to lift my end of the cot, and I was going to crawl back under the cot and apply the red stuff to all of the infected areas.

I couldn't believe it. "You want me to put my hand into that red liquid?"

Mandrake stared right into my eyes as he took my end of the cot and ordered: "Get up, Crista!"

What else could I do? I stuck my tongue out at him.

Then Mandrake and Javan lifted the cot and placed it on the sand. I told Mandrake that there was no way that I was going to stick my hand in that foul red stuff. I asked Javan if he brought any rags with him back from the village. When he said no, I looked down at my waist, around which was wrapped the remains of the captain's red sash. Untying the sash and ripping it in half, I looked in Mandrake's face and demanded: "May I use one cloth to clean the wound and the other cloth as an applicator?"

He shook his head. "Do whatever, Crista, but just do it." So I leaned over, grabbed the jar, and crawled under the captain. His leg looked worse than the foul red liquid. After I wiped the pus and blood away, Mandrake told me how to apply the red liquid gently to all of the outer edges least infected. When I first applied the liquid, cool to the captain's burning flesh, the captain flinched, almost causing me to knock over the jar.

"Be careful," Mandrake said unnecessarily. Then he told me to get the knife left near the cot. I crawled out, following Mandrake's instructions. First, I wiped that knife off on my skirt, then held it over the fire to kill any contamination. Then I crawled back under the cot and stuck the knife in the red jar. Then Mandrake told me to take the knife and scrape off the scab on the captain's knife wound. I told him I couldn't.

Mandrake gritted his teeth. "Do you remember your promise to Lilith? If you don't cut open that scab, if we can't drain some of the infection, then Captain Blackheart will either lose his leg or his life."

All I could think was, How did I get into this mess? I lifted that knife, and with one hand holding the cleaning cloth and the other hand scraping, I slowly tore off the scab. Almost the whole time, the captain was moaning and jerking his leg, and blood and pus were pouring out of the wound all over the cleaning cloth, all over my blouse, and all over my face. If I could have, I would have slapped Mandrake when he calmly said, "After most of the blood and pus exits the wound, take the other cloth, soak it in the red jar, and start cleaning out the wound."

I screamed at him. "You want me to stick my hand in that!?!"

"Of course, Crista," he replied. "It's the only way." As I gritted my teeth and soaked the cloth in the jar, Mandrake added: "Another thing, Crista. Captain Blackheart is jerking around too much. I'm afraid he may further traumatize his back. So while you are soaking his wound with that cloth, you must also reach around the cot with your other hand and hold down his leg."

That was it! I crawled out from under that cot, rose to my feet, stuck that jar of foul red liquid in Mandrake's face, and shouted, "You do it."

I wish he had shouted back at me, but instead he calmly responded, "Fine. Here, take my end of the cot."

I glared at him for several seconds, took a very deep breath, then crawled back under the cot. Within a few minutes, I was done, to Mandrake's satisfaction and mine. He told me to crawl out, empty out Lilith's bundle, and flatten the bundle on the ground next to the captain's legs. When I did so, Javan and Mandrake gently laid the captain down, with the bundle lying under his exposed right knee. Mandrake looked over at me and said, "You did a fine job, Crista." He sighed, "We have done all we can do. The captain is in the Lord's hands now."

I stretched out on my back, exhausted and feeling more unclean than I had ever felt before in my life. I looked up at the stars for awhile, then asked Mandrake, "If Captain Blackheart dies, do you think he will go to Heaven?"

Mandrake sat down next to me, likewise exhausted. "Young lady," he answered, "I have not seen much evidence that Captain Blackheart has ever trusted in the Redeemer."

Hmmm, I thought. "What does that mean?"

He took a deep breath. "Sometime soon," he replied, "I should very much like to explain. But right now, we need to attend to Lilith's body."

I looked over at Lilith's still body, wondering where she was right now. "Do you think Lilith is in Heaven now?"

Mandrake smiled and nodded. "I know she is." Mandrake and Javan took care of Lilith's body while I walked out to the beach, away from the light. I went to the water's edge and laid down on my back in the gently rolling surf. How good it was to let the water roll over me, cleansing my body of dirt, goop, blood, pus, and a foul red liquid.

*   *   *   *

When I later returned to the cot, I felt refreshed. More wood had been placed on the fire, Lilith's body was covered with many of the broad leaves, and Javan was gone. Mandrake explained that he had sent Javan back to the village to give a report on Lilith's death. I told Mandrake that I was grateful for all that he did for Captain Blackheart. He told me to get some sleep.

I lay down near the fire, cherishing its warmth, but sleep did not overtake me. I noticed that Mandrake was still sitting, so I stood, walked over to him, and sat down at his side. I looked over at the captain, then softly commented: "You never finished your story about Captain Blackheart."

*   *   *   *

For most of the rest of the night, Mandrake told me the rest of the story of Captain Blackheart. On the night that the elder and younger Blackhearts discovered that Lilith was a leper, they had an unusual visitor to their home -- Mandrake. He insisted on meeting with the captain about a very important business matter. The maid, who had been downstairs serving dinner and who had answered the door, went upstairs to inform the family of the visitor.

Of course, Lilith refused to go downstairs, and the captain was inconsolable, telling the maid to send Mandrake away. The son, eager to leave the diseased room, went downstairs to greet his erstwhile mentor. Incredibly, after several minutes, Lilith's bedroom door opened, and Mandrake walked in. Lilith wailed and hid her face, but too late to escape Mandrake's observation. The captain, outraged at this violation of privacy, drew his sword and ordered Mandrake to leave the bedroom. Mandrake stood his ground, telling the captain that the purpose of his unexpected and unwelcomed visit was to discuss a plan that could save his wife's life.

The captain let down his guard, perplexed at how Mandrake or anyone else could possibly have known that his wife had contracted leprosy. Mandrake's explanation was simple and forthcoming. Mandrake's only child, a cute, bright-eyed, five-year-old boy who was the spitting image of his mother, had likewise recently developed leprosy. The captain extended his condolences, then asked why Mandrake traveled all the way from the City of Cain to Livernium to tell him of his family problems.

Mandrake's explanation was dreadful. Largely because of his son's medical condition, Cain was considering a proposal that all lepers would be condemned to death by burning at the stake. Lilith began to wail again, and the captain drew his sword again, threatening to kill Cain. Mandrake told him to put away his sword. Mandrake needed the captain to help him appeal to Cain not to issue such a decree.

The captain quickly agreed, and taking leave of his wife, went downstairs to meet with Mandrake and the captain's son to prepare for the trip and also to prepare a backup plan in the event that their appeal was unsuccessful. The younger Blackheart was too numb to contribute much to the planning. He was still conflicted with natural affection for his mother, but natural revulsion for her condition. He objected strongly to the backup plan, but finally relented under direct orders from his father.

Mandrake and the elder captain wasted no time leaving for the City of Cain. Both men were known to Cain, Mandrake more than the captain, and within a few hours of arrival in the city, Cain agreed to meet with them at his mansion. During that waiting period, Mandrake hurried home to greet his wife and son and to start executing the backup plan, if needed.

Later that afternoon, Cain, attended by the then chief priest Theron and a squad of priestly guards, listened attentively to the special plea of two men anxious to save the lives of their loved ones. At the conclusion of their statements, Theron whispered something to Cain, who then offered to make them one concession: the leper could die in his own home, burned at the stake in the common room, achieving two worthy goals of destroying not only diseased flesh but also a diseased house.

The captain's flaming temper betrayed him one final time. Unsheathing and flashing his sword, the captain screamed that he would kill Cain. Moments later, the sword dropped harmlessly to the floor, the captain's body pierced through with many spears. Mandrake himself, standing next to the captain, escaped death only because of the accuracy of the guards. As the body was being taken away and the blood wiped from the marble floor, Cain announced that he would be merciful -- the decree would take effect the following day, giving Mandrake and his wife Naamah time to say goodbye to their son.

When he was released from the mansion, Mandrake flew home to execute his backup plan. He pounded three stakes into the floor of the common room of his small home near the south gate of the city. Then he brought in from the courtyard the skeletons of three pigs which he had purchased and butchered just that afternoon. He piled the skeleton of each pig -- one small pig, one medium pig, and one large pig -- around the respective stakes, piling the rest of the butchered pig remains atop the skeletons. Then, Mandrake brought in yards and yards of wood which he had collected in a spare bedroom, piling wood at the feet and all around each stake. Then he brought in kindling and spread it around each stake. After that, he brought into the common room nearly every wooden item in the house, placing all of that fuel as close to the stakes as possible.

By that time, the sun had gone down, and the streets were emptying out. Mandrake and his family, taking only a few special belongings and wearing cloaks with hoods upon them, walked out of the back door of the house, made their way through an alley to the main street, and then calmly strolled down the street and out the south gate. Several hundred yards away, the trio turned off the road and headed toward a thicket about a quarter of a mile from the road. There, Mandrake placed his wife and son on the front seat of a wagon, with one fresh horse ready to travel. In the back of the wagon were clothes, bedrolls, food, water, and special family treasures, including some of Mandrake's precious books from his many years of teaching at the School of Humanism.

With his family settled, Mandrake returned home. He struck a match and lit each pile of kindling. When he was satisfied that the kindling had caught, and that each pile of wood was burning, he dashed out the back door; sauntering through the alley and down the main street, he soon rejoined his family. Hiding his wife and son in the back of the wagon with the supplies, Mandrake slowly edged the horse and wagon out of the thicket. When he reached the road, he turned south and continued very slowly, careful not to attract attention or to harm the horse or wagon. When he reached the first junction, he turned left and headed slowly southeast toward Livernium.

Mandrake never knew if his ruse worked completely, but regardless, Cain was satisfied when he received news the next morning from Theron that Mandrake and Naamah and their son had all perished in a house fire the night before. The rest of Mandrake and Naamah's families were notified of their untimely death; and soon, their memory receded in the busy lives of most of the occupants of the city and of the students at the School of Humanism.

*　　*　　*　　*

Two weeks later, when they reached Livernium, Mandrake drove the wagon straight to the docks. The younger Blackheart was alone aboard ship, with only one other crew member -- a vulgar old sea salt named Letch. All of the other crew members had grumbled but accepted the simple story that the *Lucky Lady* would only need a skeleton crew to make a special cruise for the captain and his family. Young Blackheart kept an eye on the docks and ordered Letch to inspect the lines and rigging while Mandrake stowed the special passengers and cargo into the captain's cabin.

When all was loaded, the younger Blackheart insisted that Mandrake give him an explanation for his father's absence. The younger Blackheart closed his eyes, pondered the unfairness of the world and his abhorrence of leprosy, and lamented his father's evil temper. He looked up at Mandrake, who again said he was sorry, and then commented: "That eventuality was part of father's backup plan."

He ordered Letch to prepare to sail, and then young Blackheart drove the wagon back to his house. His mother was waiting, her outfit covered by a cloak with a hood. Taking care not to yet tell his mother of her husband's passing, and taking care not to get too close to his diseased mother, young Blackheart made his mother climb into the back of the wagon, where she rode to the docks. Upon arrival, Mandrake left the cabin, walked down the gangplank, and helped Lilith out of the wagon and into the captain's cabin. The younger Blackheart drove the horse and wagon to a blacksmith shop, where he boarded the horse with instructions that he would be back within a week. Then, he walked back to the dock, boarded the *Lucky Lady*, and ordered Letch to shove off.

* * * *

The *Lucky Lady* took four days to sail to an island far out in the Great Sea, far away from the normal shipping channels that generally hugged the seacoast. That island was known in the sailing community as Leper Island, a God-forsaken place where family members dropped off and deserted other family members who had leprosy. During the entire trip, only Mandrake left the cabin, and only when he had to help with sailing chores or cooking. Letch eyed the whole situation suspiciously, especially that the stranger Mandrake was doing the cooking for the cabin guests and that young Blackheart refused to go near the captain's cabin. But Letch asked no questions, only guessing at the ultimate destination of this special cruise.

When the ship arrived off the coast of the island, the younger Blackheart ordered Letch to anchor near the only decent beach on the island. The other passengers and cargo were offloaded by Mandrake in the dinghy. When Mandrake came back with the dinghy after the final offload, Mandrake asked the captain if he wanted to come ashore and say a final farewell to his mother. Refusing to come near anyone with leprosy, the captain waved Mandrake off, and as Mandrake swam to shore and the ship turned to sail back to Livernium, young Blackheart looked back one last time, waved to his mother, and never saw her again.

Chapter Twenty-two

A New Day

When Mandrake finished telling me the story, I started to cry, not for the tragic events in Captain Blackheart's life, but because I missed my mother so much. I would have given anything to see her and hug her. And yet, lying near my feet was a man who spurned his mother's attention and affection, a man who did everything in his power to not see her again, to not hug her again. "He never came back to see his mother, did he, Mandrake?" I asked softly.

"Never," he answered. "The last thing he told me aboard ship was that he never wanted to be in the presence of a leper for the rest of his life."

*   *   *   *

My thoughts turned back to that last cruise. "Didn't Letch suspect anything?" I asked.

"Of course," Mandrake explained. "It was definitely tense aboard ship. One day I overheard the captain tell Letch that, if he finished the cruise and kept his mouth shut, he would be promoted to first mate. Then I heard Letch bargaining with the captain, pointing out that the captain could make him first mate for one trip, then demote him back to sailor." Mandrake shook his head. "Those two had a few heated words until the captain agreed that as long as he did a good job, Letch would be the first mate as long as he lived."

I thought about the captain's bargain, then looked at his bruised and battered body. Mandrake remarked, "This slave trader has more than his share of faults, but I'll grant you this, Crista. He was a man of his word. Letch was his first mate . . . as long as he lived."

*   *   *   *

Mandrake looked over at me and asked, "Are you planning on getting any sleep tonight, young lady? The sun will rise soon."

I stared into the fire, wondering about all of the things that had happened to the captain and me in the last few weeks, wondering why some people lived and some people died. I looked over at Mandrake and said, "If you're ready, I am."

"Ready to sleep?" he asked hopefully.

"No, sir," I answered. "Ready to hear about that Redeemer you talked about earlier. I remember my Daddy talking about a Redeemer, though I never really listened very well." I paused, then added, "I'm thinking I'm ready to listen now."

Mandrake folded his hands together, got up and put some logs on the fire, and then sat down next to me. Then he politely asked me if he could pray.

"Please do," I hurriedly agreed. "Pray for me and the captain . . ." and then as my thoughts strayed overseas, "and for my Daddy, if he is still alive, and for my mother, and even for my brother Methuselah." I felt so relieved as Mandrake started to pray, then so surprised that he prayed to God like he was talking to a personal friend sitting next to him on the beach.

When he finished praying, I opened my eyes and stared into the fire as Mandrake started telling me another story, this one about a sneaking, scheming Satan who deceived Eve into committing the First Calamitous Sin. When I blurted out that I had heard that Tale of Father Adam before, Mandrake corrected me: "Crista, I am not telling you a make-believe story made up by a man. I am telling you the very Words of God."

"Oh," I said in an apologetic tone. "Go on."

And he did. Part of the curse brought upon Adam and Eve for violating God's commandment was that they were banished from the Garden of Eden, where they could have lived forever in a glorious paradise and in perfect fellowship with God. But God cannot abide in the presence of sin. Their sin separated Adam and Eve from fellowship with God. Cast out into the world, Adam and Eve faced a life, and death, without God.

"You see, Crista," he explained. "The wages of sin is death, just as Lilith died tonight. And if a person dies in his sins, he will be separated from God for eternity."

That didn't sound like a good bargain to me, so I asked, "What can I do to have my sins taken away so I can have fellowship with this God of yours?"

Mandrake explained that there was nothing I could do, but that God had promised a Redeemer Who would take our sins upon Him, Who would do what we could not so that we could go where we otherwise could not go.

I shook my head and asked Mandrake if he could clear things up for me. Then he asked me a couple of simple questions which I could answer easily. "Crista, do you think that Letch was a sinner?"

"He was an evil, wicked man," I quickly answered.

"When he died at the mouth of a shark in the Great Sea, do you think that Letch went to Heaven?"

"I doubt it, Mandrake."

"Good answers," he said. "You see, Crista, death and the Devil are like that great white shark that Letch met at the end of his life." I shivered at the vision of such a death without God.

*   *   *   *

Then Mandrake started asking me more difficult questions. "Crista, do you think that you are a sinner?"

"Hmmm," I replied, thinking back over my life. "I'm not as bad as Letch was."

Mandrake laughed. "I hope not, at your age." Then he asked me if I had ever lied, ever cheated, ever stolen anything, ever disobeyed my parents. After I nodded my head, he described the effects of sin in our life. "Sin is like leprosy. Once it takes root, you can never get rid of it. Sin spreads over your body, destroying your soul just as leprosy destroys your body." Then he made another comparison. "Sin is like the captain's dagger. It doesn't matter how deep the wound is, sin spreads its poison, infecting other areas of your life. God can't let people into Heaven if their souls are infected with sin. That sin would spread to other areas of Heaven, and then Heaven wouldn't be Heaven anymore."

*   *   *   *

I pondered Mandrake's words for a few moments before he asked me another question. "Crista, if you had died on the *Lucky Lady*, or in the mouth of a shark, or in a dinghy out in the middle of the sea, or on a rock off the shore of Leper Island, do you think that you would have gone to Heaven?"

I was starting to make a connection. God wouldn't let Letch infect Heaven with his big sins, and God wouldn't let me infect Heaven with my smaller sins. "I guess not," I answered honestly.

"Good answer, Crista," he replied. "Now, you are ready to hear about the Redeemer." Mandrake started explaining that God promised Adam and Eve that He would send the Seed of Woman to battle the Devil for the souls of mankind. The Devil would wound the Redeemer in the heel, but the Redeemer would ultimately win, wounding the Devil in his head.

"Crista," Mandrake further explained, "I want you to think back to your battle with the sharks. What would have happened to Captain Blackheart if you had not been with him in the dinghy?"

"That's easy," I answered. "The sharks would have devoured him."

"Precisely," Mandrake continued. "The captain was absolutely helpless to save himself from those sharks. Now, how was the captain saved?"

"I stuck that dagger into the shark's snout."

"Exactly. That was the only way that the captain could have been saved. Somebody else had to save him. Somebody else had to risk his life to face that shark alone. Somebody else had to bravely take that dagger and stab the shark in the head."

Now I was starting to understand. Mandrake finished his comparison. "Crista, think of yourself as wounded by sin, helpless, lying in that dinghy, as Satan the Shark streaks toward you, eager to devour your soul. There is absolutely nothing you can do to save your life. Suddenly, the Redeemer is at your side. He battles the shark, and the shark wounds the Redeemer's heel. But in the end, the Redeemer takes out His dagger and stabs the shark's snout, wounding its head, defeating it. That's what our Redeemer will do for us one day."

*   *   *   *

Mandrake paused, raised his arms to the sky, and softly said, "Blessed be the name of the Lord." Then he explained some things that I had never before considered when I heard my father tell the Tales of Father Adam. "Crista, the Devil is going to rejoice when he wounds the heel of the Redeemer; but what the Devil doesn't realize is that the only way that the Redeemer could win that battle is to shed His precious blood when He is wounded in the heel. Crista," he explained, "the only thing that can cleanse our soul from the infection of sin is the blood of the Redeemer."

He then described how I felt when he asked me to apply the foul red liquid to the captain's wounds. "You didn't want to do it, Crista, but you went ahead and did it because you cared so much for the captain. And you had made a promise to Lilith that you would take care of her son, no matter what the price." As I nodded my head, Mandrake continued, "If you had not applied the red liquid, the captain would have no hope of his infection ever being cured." He paused, sighed, and continued: "One day, Crista, the Redeemer is going to shed His precious blood for our sins, covering the infection of our soul, and cleansing us from all unrighteousness."

It made so much sense, but how could I be sure? "How can you be so sure of all this, Mandrake?" I asked.

He smiled and quickly answered: "Because the Words of God say so."

*   *   *   *

So I pondered that answer. "Well," I asked, "assuming I believe that the Words of God are true, how do I get the infection of my soul cleansed?"

"Crista," Mandrake repeated, "the Words of God are true, and there is nothing that you or I can do to cleanse our soul's infection. Just as Captain Blackheart was in no condition to apply the foul red liquid to his wound tonight, we are not in a position to cleanse ourselves. Someone else has to apply that red liquid, and the only Person Who can apply His blood to cleanse us from our sins is the Redeemer."

That started making sense. "Well then, Mandrake, supposing I believe that the Redeemer is going to shed His blood for my sins, what else do I have to do to uhh, be, uhh, saved from my sins?"

"Just trust in the Redeemer, Crista. Just as you clung to that rock last night, believing that it would save you from drowning, just cling to the Redeemer, the Solid Rock, the only One Who can save you from drowning in your sins." As I thought about his words, Mandrake went back to the rock. "Remember last night when you were slipping off that rock? The only way you were saved was that the captain gave you a nudge. The captain didn't save you; the rock did; but the captain gave you a nudge to cling to the rock."

As my thoughts went back to that fateful nudge, when a man who could not even move his legs was willing to sacrifice his life to give me that nudge, Mandrake pleaded with me. "That's all I can do tonight, Crista. I can't save you. Only the Solid Rock can save you. All I can do is give you that nudge."

It all came together. I finally understood that I was a sinner, and that my sin was infecting my soul, making me unfit for Heaven. I finally understood that the Redeemer was going to shed His precious blood, which would cleanse me from all my unrighteousness. I finally understood with my head, and now Mandrake was nudging me to cling to the Rock.

I felt a compelling tug on my heart. All I wanted was to have that fellowship that Mandrake had with God, both now and for eternity. I wanted to see Lilith again. I bowed my head, and in my own clumsy words, I asked the Redeemer to take away my sins and save my soul.

*　　*　　*　　*

When I opened my eyes, Mandrake saw a gleam that was not there before. He whispered, "Praise God." Then I noticed that the first rays of sunlight were shining in the sky overhead. I smiled at Mandrake and rejoiced: "It's a new day."

Chapter Twenty-three

A Very Difficult Patient

Mandrake and I walked down to the water and watched the sunrise while waiting for the others to come from the village. After a few minutes, we heard a familiar, cultured voice. "Excuse me. Could I please get some water?"

We both turned to look at the captain, eyes pleading for us to help him slake his thirst. When he saw Mandrake approaching, the captain spoke again. "I knew it had to be you. So you are still alive?"

Mandrake smiled, purposefully waved his left hand in greeting, then shrugged: "I didn't expect to see you again, Captain Blackheart."

I chuckled, but the captain didn't. "Don't come near me, Mandrake."

Mandrake stopped dead in the sand, and so did I. "As you wish, Captain Blackheart."

When I didn't move, the captain ordered me to get him some water. I glanced at Mandrake, who motioned for me to comply. I went to the jug, scooped up some water with the cup, and slowly poured its contents into the captain's mouth. Then, when the captain's thirst was satiated, for the moment, Mandrake spoke again. "I am sorry to inform you, Captain, that for the sake of your survival, I was compelled to conduct certain medical procedures upon your body."

The captain gasped. "You mean that you touched my body!?!" he shrieked.

"As little as possible," Mandrake replied. "Crista did most of the actual procedures, under my direction, of course."

"Well," the captain grumbled, "it didn't help. I feel terrible."

"Good," Mandrake replied. "The fact that you are feeling pain indicates that your body is recovering."

"No," the captain corrected him. "The fact that I am feeling pain indicates that I feel horrible."

"As you wish, Captain," Mandrake replied with a smile.

The captain moaned for a few moments, then looked at me. "I guess you didn't obey my last command, young lady."

I smiled down at him. "If you mean that I did not flee, you are correct. I promised that I would never leave you or forsake you, remember? And besides," I added, "where was I going to go?"

"You could have drowned both of us in the sea," the captain suggested.

"I was too tired to carry you anymore," I replied.

Mandrake smiled, but the captain was not amused. In fact, he didn't find much of anything humorous that morning, especially after Mandrake gave him a report of his physical condition. The captain looked at Mandrake and asked, "Mandrake, are you a praying man?"

Mandrake was surprised at the question. "I never was before, but yes, since I have been here on Leper Island, I have become a praying man."

"Good," the captain said. "Pray that I die from either the infection or my broken back."

I giggled.

Then Mandrake became serious. "There is another thing that I have not mentioned yet, Captain Blackheart."

"Will it kill me?" the captain asked expectantly.

"I doubt it, Captain." Then Mandrake explained the difficulty that he was having in examining and treating his right knee. "Fortunately, Crista and I had the assistance of two other people."

As much as possible, the captain's head slumped. "Don't tell me, Mandrake, that you allowed two other lepers near me?"

"It was the only way that we could get to your knee. One of the other persons was Javan."

"Great!" the captain exclaimed. "What does your son look like now?"

I gasped. "Mandrake, you never told me that Javan was your son."

"You never asked." Then, turning back to the captain, he said that the other person was Lilith.

The captain's eyes closed, and he fell silent for over a minute. When he finally spoke, his jaw was tight. "I thought I told you that I never wanted to see her hideous face again."

"Don't worry, Captain," Mandrake replied. "You won't."

"Good!" the captain exhaled. "Did she go back to the village last night?"

Mandrake lowered his eyes, sighed, and then looked right into the captain's eyes. "Captain Blackheart, I am saddened to inform you that your mother passed away last night here on the beach, dying in the act of trying to save her son's life."

* * * *

Captain Blackheart stared vacantly up into the sky for a few moments, then asked where her body was. When Mandrake said that her body lay just a few feet away, the captain vainly attempted to move around to see his mother's earthly body. But he spotted something that I had taken out of his mother's bundle -- a small, wooden ship, a mere child's toy that Lilith had given to her son on his fifth birthday, shortly before his father had taken her son away to live in the City of Cain.

The younger Blackheart forgot to pack his toy boat when he moved away at age five. And he didn't remember it when he returned home at age ten. But now, at age forty, the memories came flooding over him, and he wept until the pain of weeping caused him to lose consciousness.

* * * *

Javan, along with a small group of villagers, reappeared shortly thereafter with a crude coffin and burial clothes for Lilith. The party also brought a variety of foods and other household supplies. When I asked

Mandrake what they were for, he explained that the captain could not be moved very far in his present condition and that I was to stay with him near the beach as a nurse during his convalescence.

As the party prepared to return to the village for the funeral, the captain regained consciousness. Hearing movement and voices around him, he shouted, "Keep those people away from me, Mandrake!" Mandrake bit his lip and told the captain that they were just leaving for his mother's funeral.

My heart broke when the captain replied, "Good." As the party began to leave, I walked up to the captain, looked down in his face, and told him that I would be back after the funeral.

The captain shrieked, "NO!" Mandrake stopped his party and came back to the cot. "What's wrong, Captain?"

He composed himself. "Please explain to Crista that she cannot go to the village for any purpose, including my mother's funeral."

Mandrake turned to me and said flatly, "Crista, the captain does not want you to go to the village for any purpose, including his mother's funeral."

The captain saw the uncertainty in my eyes. "Crista, you must not go to the village. You must not get near these people. I am trying to protect you."

Mandrake waited for my decision. I looked at the men holding aloft the coffin of Lilith, and then I turned back to look at the captain. "Begging your pardon, sir, but the only way we could save your life last night was for me to get close, very close, to these people."

The captain pleaded with me.   "Crista, you promised to not leave me or forsake me."

I looked down at the man with both pity and disgust.   "I'll be back soon.   If Lilith's son can't go to his mother's funeral, her sister will."

The captain blinked his eyes, then exclaimed, "My mother doesn't have a sister."

As I turned to walk away, I corrected the captain. "She does now."

*   *   *   *

I can honestly state that Lilith's funeral was the first leper funeral I had ever attended.   The captain was right.   Most of the people at the cemetery, located south and just downhill of the village, were in various stages of hideous.   Most of them were also in various stages of mourning, and really were not all that interested in the new arrival on the island.

Mandrake did introduce me to his wife Naamah -- a beautiful, graceful brunette who did not appear to have one vestige of leprosy about her.   Many years ago they had taken in a five-year-old boy.   I wondered if they would take in a twelve-year-old girl.

The funeral service was a simple graveside service.   The grave had been dug earlier in the morning.   Before lowering the casket, Mandrake spoke briefly about the curse of sin.   "Wherefore, as by one man sin entered into the world, and death by sin; and so death passed upon all men, for that all have sinned." He comforted us with the words that though the wages of sin is death, the gift of God is eternal life through the

Redeemer, Who would one day come to Earth to shed His precious blood to provide a covering for our sins, and that all who would cling to Him would be saved from the penalty of sin. He comforted many when he said that he knew that Lilith had gone to Heaven.

And then Mandrake gave a benediction. "The Lord giveth, and the Lord taketh away. Blessed be the name of the Lord." In a kind act, he briefly told the people that shortly after the Lord took Lilith away to Heaven, the Lord gave new life to a young lady recently shipwrecked on the island. For the rest of my life, I will always remember Lilith's funeral service. And for the rest of my life, I will look forward to seeing Lilith again.

*   *   *   *

After the funeral service, Mandrake organized a work party to carry all sorts of building materials back to the beach. He explained to me that it was useless to attempt to get Captain Blackheart to agree to live in the village, and that it would be better for the village dwellers if they did not have to be within earshot of the captain's derisive comments about lepers. When Mandrake further explained that I had to also live at the beach to take care of the captain in his condition, my heart was filled with so many emotions that Mandrake paused from his efficient organizational efforts to ask me if I had any problem with the arrangement.

I looked up at him and asked how long the captain was going to be in his present condition. Mandrake didn't know. As I thought about my earlier promise to the captain that I would not leave him or forsake him, I realized that I had placed no time limits on that vow. And besides, I promised Lilith that I would take care of her son. While I might have been tempted to break my promise to the captain, I was not going to break my promise to his mother.

Then I asked Mandrake if anyone else was going to help me. I mean, by God's grace I was able to help the captain out in an emergency situation or two. But the task of caring for the captain all alone, day after day, week after week, month after month, maybe year after year, maybe decade after decade, maybe century after century, well, I was getting a little overwhelmed. Mandrake was firm. "I realize that the task is imposing, but if God has laid this task upon you, then He will give you the grace to perform it." Then he smiled. "Frankly, Crista," he joked, "if I had to do this job, I would choke that irritating man within a week."

After envisioning the glee which many slaves would have in choking the captain, I still insisted to Mandrake that I would need regular help. His brow furrowed as he pondered this dilemma. Mandrake knew that the captain would only allow non-lepers to care for him. "Such complications," Mandrake mused aloud. "Let me consult my wife." Then he took a brief break while I munched on a loaf of bread which one of the others had given to me.

Mandrake and his wife returned shortly. She was carrying a bundle upon her shoulders. Mandrake briefly explained that Naamah would assist me temporarily in taking care of the captain. When I protested his decision, Naamah spoke up in the most pleasant voice. "Crista,

I am the only other person on the island who does not have leprosy. Besides," she added, "I have taken care of young Blackheart before. If anyone can handle him, I can." I finally relented in my opposition to separating a man from his wife when Mandrake assured me that his wife would spend weekends back at the village.

It was also decided that two small huts would have to be built near the beach -- one for the captain and the other for the ladies. When everything was together, Mandrake led a large party back to the beach.

*   *   *   *

As we neared the end of the path to the beach, I was shocked. The captain was not on his cot.

Many thoughts and emotions instantly swelled up inside of me. But then Mandrake cried out, "There he is!" I looked further down the beach, and there was the captain, lying on his stomach, crawling with his hands and useless feet toward the surf. He almost made it. Mandrake, several of the men, and I dashed to the captain's side. The captain started crying out, "Don't touch me! Let me die! Don't touch me! Let me die!" Mandrake ordered two men to bring the cot, and as gently as they could, they lifted the captain, thrashing all the way, upon the cot.

While they were walking the captain back up the beach, Mandrake cheerily said: "What excellent progress you are making, Captain Blackheart." The captain clamped his mouth shut. Looking down on him, I added to his misery. "You are so pitiful." He spat back: "I don't want your pity. All I want to do is die."

I spat back. "Begging your pardon, sir, all I meant is that if you had not pulled that stunt of trying to drown yourself in the sea, then you would not have had to be manhandled by a group of lepers." The captain clamped his mouth shut when I finished my statement. "If you don't let me take care of you, then the lepers will."

Naamah turned to her husband and laughed: "Perhaps I am not needed after all. Crista seems to handle the captain quite well by herself."

*   *   *   *

It took two days to put up two huts and get our new settlement in order. Of course, the captain either complained or clamped his mouth shut the whole time that the lepers were anywhere near him. When Mandrake explained to the captain that Naamah would be helping me take care of him for awhile, the captain spat: "I don't need a nanny."

Within a few days, Naamah and I settled into a routine of getting the water, picking fruit, baking flat bread on a skillet over the open fire, cleaning the captain's wounds and bruises, and worst of all, changing his soiled clothing.

The captain never became comfortable with that latter indignity. And it took him quite awhile to accept the other changes in his life -- his beard and hair were turning gray, and his hair started falling out. When I first pointed it out to him, the captain replied: "Nonsense! My father had a black beard and a full head of black hair until the day he died." When I mentioned a week later that his hair looked even more gray, he continued to deny the possibility. I brought Naamah into his hut, and she informed the captain that I was sadly correct. I offered the possibility that perhaps his body was reacting to the poison that may still have been in his system. The captain latched on to that explanation, assuring himself that his hair would soon be back to its natural black brilliance. That was the first time I had ever realized that men could be as vain as women.

$$* \quad * \quad * \quad *$$

Naamah and I also settled into the daily routine of hearing the captain complain and sulk, wishing one moment that he were dead, then hoping the next moment that a ship would rescue him, then whining that a crippled man could never captain a ship, then hoping that he would walk again someday. I developed another routine of giving the captain a scorecard each evening: No, sir, you didn't die today; No, sir, a ship hasn't rescued you yet; No, sir, you didn't walk today; Yes, sir, your hair is turning grayer. He was not amused.

Chapter Twenty-four

Naamah

One of the greatest blessings during my time on Leper Island was getting to know Naamah and Mandrake. Mercifully, the captain's body, in its long, slow healing process, required a great deal of rest. During those hours, while we sat on the beach or in the hut, Naamah would ask me about my family, and I would ask about hers. She showed keen interest in the shepherd's life and the life of a shepherd's wife, since she had been raised in the city. I told her that I wished that she could meet my parents and brother one day. She became wistful, then assured me that if she did not meet them here on Earth, that she hoped to see them in Heaven.

I told Naamah about Adah and our shared dream of finding careers in the City of Gom. Naamah frowned whenever I mentioned Adah's name. She told me that all she ever wanted to be was a wife and mother; and though she had attained both in the City of Cain, she said that she never wanted to move back. "I have my family with me, and I have found peace and the Lord here on Leper Island, Crista," she smiled. "What more could a woman want?"

One afternoon, escaping the cruel sun and sitting in the coolness of the trees, I asked her about her childhood. A little frown appeared on her face, and she replied, "It was not peaceful." Then she asked me if I had ever heard of a man named Lamech, or as he was called later, Lamech-Cain. When I confessed my ignorance, Naamah started talking about her father, describing him as a tall, handsome man with blue eyes and long golden locks, a very intelligent man who founded the School of Humanism in the City of Cain. He was also a very cultured man, expressing interest in all branches of knowledge, especially animal husbandry, music and the arts, and scientific progress. His natural leadership skills eventually brought him to the attention of Cain himself, who molded her father into Lamech-Cain and made him one of the city leaders.

She described her father as a man who could be very charming and who was able to cleverly disguise his lust for power. "My father appeared in public as a loyal deputy to Cain, but at home, he talked much with his family about his desire to succeed Cain whenever Cain passed away. Indeed, my father despised Cain's religious cult as much as Captain Blackheart despises lepers."

"Whew!" I replied.

"My father spent much time planning his succession, even to the point of changing his name to eliminate any association with Cain. He finally settled on the name Saaga as a name worthy of a brilliant leader. His obsession with succession was so great that he even told his wife and children that we should call him Lamech-Cain in public, but Saaga at home. But he warned us that the name of Saaga was a tightly guarded family secret. No one outside of the family could ever know about the name Saaga until my father actually ascended to power in the City of Cain after Cain's death."

"Wow!" I blurted out. "I don't think I would want to get into a succession battle with your father."

"Yes," Naamah said, "Saaga enjoyed the battle of wits with other city leaders. Indeed, as time went on, the only other leader close to Cain was the chief priest of the cult of the Great Ebony Cow."

At the mention of the chief priest of Cain's cult, my mind raced back to the night I was saved, when Mandrake spent hours telling me the story of Captain Blackheart. "Theron," I blurted out. "Wasn't his name Theron?"

Wrinkles appeared on Naamah's face at the mention of Theron's name. "I guess," I said apologetically, "that you don't like to hear the name of the man who suggested to Cain that your son be burned at the stake."

"Actually, Crista," Naamah responded with a very deep breath, "burning lepers at the stake was someone else's suggestion first."

Since this conversation and Naamah's countenance were turning dark, I tried to steer the conversation back to Naamah's childhood. I asked her if she had any brothers or sisters. "Yes," she sighed again, "my father is very proud of his three sons, but not so proud of me."

I was getting frustrated that I was not able to find a topic of conversation that was not troubling to Naamah. She sensed my frustration and said, "Although we did not always get along very well, I was proud of my brothers, too." So she started to talk with some enthusiasm about Jabal, Jubal, and Tubal-cain, all of whom shared their father's intellect and love of learning. "My oldest brother was Jabal," she explained, a wistful smile curling her lips. "When he was younger, he loved animals."

When I responded that I loved cuddly lambs and that I hated it when Daddy sacrificed one at the family altar, Naamah laughed easily. "Crista, Jabal's childhood interest in cuddly lambs or any other animals was eventually replaced by a purely scientific curiosity. As for sacrificing animals on the family altar, I can assure you that we never had any such sacrifices in my home."

Naamah continued her family history. "Crista, when you told me about your father and his revulsion at people eating roast cow, I'm afraid that practice started with my family." She explained that Theron and Cain worked out the details for the cult of the Great Ebony Cow, but that Saaga, the founder of the School of Humanism, would have nothing to do with worshipping cows. However, her father did develop the very practical business idea of selling the sacrificed cow to other people to eat. "Your father is the one behind meat eating!?!" I blurted out. "Yes, Crista," Naamah said sadly, "and Father placed Jabal in charge of developing ever improving varieties of beef cattle."

I closed my eyes, recalling the time that Methuselah brought Daddy home in a daze, defeated at the gate of the City of Gom in a losing battle to keep meat eating out of the city. And here, on Leper Island, I was learning how meat eating came about. My mind turned back to Naamah. "Tell me about your second brother."

Naamah's eyes danced with delight when talking about Jubal, the father of all such as handle the harp and organ. "Jubal loved music. He was always singing around the house, day and night. Nobody could shut him up. And when he was older, he passed on his love for music to me and taught me how to sing." When I asked if Jubal sang the songs of Father Adam that I was familiar with, Naamah shook her head. "We were never allowed to sing those songs in the house of the founder of the School of Humanism."

Naamah then explained that her father encouraged Jubal to invent new musical instruments and to instruct others how to play. "Father would often say that music was a wonderful device to lift the spirit of man to greater heights of glory." She then explained how her father helped Jubal start the School of Music in the City of Cain, a place where boys and girls and young men and women could develop their skills to the highest level.

Naamah was really warming up now. When I asked about her third brother, her face broke out into a big grin. "Ahh, Tubal-cain!" When I told her that one my father's playmates growing up was a man named Tubal, Naamah beamed. "My brother Tubal-cain was my favorite playmate growing up." Naamah described all of the times that she and Tubal-cain went exploring in the City of Cain, dashing from shop to shop in the marketplace, playing games in the city street. While she was talking, my heart and mind went back to my father's homestead, where I had spent my childhood playing with Methuselah, running and laughing in the garden, plopping into a pumpkin, making up a Pumpkinhead song. All of a sudden, I was very homesick.

Naamah continued to tell me about her brother. "Tubal-cain was very good with his hands, very inventive. Father hired a blacksmith and rented a building where Tubal-cain could experiment with various metals to make them stronger or more pliable. Of course, Father started both a business and a school where Tubal-cain could instruct others in making artful brass decorations and stronger iron tools such as sturdier and sharper plows." Then her countenance darkened as she explained how her father and Cain had also commissioned Tubal-cain to make stronger brass shields and sharper spears and swords.

*   *   *   *

Then Naamah giggled. She explained that she was such a disappointment to her father because all she was interested in was dolls and playing with her brothers. She was interested in cute and cuddly animals, but she didn't have the discipline to learn how to play one of her brother's musical instruments. "And," she laughed, "unlike you and your friend Adah, I had no interest in working in a blacksmith shop with my brother. Blacksmith shops are hot and dirty, with foul fumes in the air. Whenever Father would ask me what I wanted to be when I grew up, I always answered that all I wanted to be was a wife and mother. That answer sent Father into a rage. He insisted that we children strive diligently to improve ourselves, our culture, and mankind." When I commented that I thought that was a noble ideal, Naamah looked at me sternly. "People have taken that noble ideal too far."

*   *   *   *

Naamah seemed to be getting upset again, so I asked Naamah about her mother. She smiled as she told me about Zillah, an unusual combination of raving beauty and brilliant intellect. As I wondered what her mother was like, Naamah continued. "Of course, Mother was Father's second wife."

My heart went out to poor Naamah and to Saaga. How sad it must be to lose your wife. I gently asked, "How did your father's first wife die?"

Naamah shook her head. "As far as I know, she is still alive."

Now that was confusing. I stared into Naamah's eyes, trying to make sense of her words. I mean, when God gave Eve to Adam, it was for life. When Enoch took Sarah's hand in marriage, it was for life. The only way a man could possibly have a second wife is for the first wife to die, right?

My mind whirled. Was it possible for a man to get rid of his wife? How cruel that would be! How horrible that would be to their children! Surely men could not become so heartless, so vile, as to get rid of their wife.

Naamah did not want me to be confused. "Crista, wherever your imagination is taking your mind right now, you could not possibly guess the truth." So I stopped thinking, but kept staring. "Father was first married to a woman named Adah, yes, the same name as your friend. Adah is, in her own way, a wonderful woman, a lovely blonde with a voice that was said to be the most beautiful singing voice that people ever heard. She had a radiant spirit, bringing joy everywhere she went."

"What happened to her?" I asked.

"Adah's only mistake was that she stopped bearing children after Jubal was born. Father had dreams of populating the Earth with many children who would be as handsome, as intelligent, as cultured as he was. So, after a few years, when Adah did not have any more children, he married a young woman named Zillah."

I gasped. "While he was still married to Adah?"

Naamah sighed. "I was not there, of course, at the time, but I heard how Father justified his actions to his students at the School of Humanism. He was so proud of himself for his new idea, for his newest freedom, for his newest flaunting of the Words of God."

I tried to shake the cobwebs out of my head. "Why did Zillah ever agree to marry a man who was already married?"

Naamah nodded her head. "That's a question I asked my mother after I was older." Then Naamah described how her mother, a star pupil at the School of Humanism, was overwhelmed, as were most other young ladies, by Lamech-Cain's handsome face and charming ways. She had a crush on her teacher, and when Lamech-Cain suggested that they marry, she was swept off of her feet.

"What about Zillah's father?" I blurted out. "Surely he protested this terrible violation of all that is decent."

"Very simply," Naamah explained, "Father paid him off."

I became jittery, feeling unclean, talking about such wicked things. I wondered how all of this made Adah feel. "As you can imagine, Adah was outraged at this horrible insult to her dignity and to her children.

She was too good a woman to leave her husband, and besides, she had nowhere else to go. But the radiance went out in her eyes, and the joy went out of her voice. I never heard her sing, and I never saw her smile."

I had trouble believing such a story. "Your family life must have been a mess, Naamah."

"To say the least," she replied. "Adah never had a kind word to say to my mother, though Zillah tried to be pleasant to her. Adah never accepted that she no longer had first place in her husband's heart."

"What about your father?" I asked. "Didn't he find such a household arrangement unsatisfying?" Naamah then explained that her father rarely spent time at home, busy as he was with his School of Humanism, helping to advise Cain on city matters, and helping his sons start their own schools and businesses.

A tear formed in Naamah's eye, and then she began to softly cry, and then her body became wracked with sobs. I leaned over and held her, thinking I understood. I ventured a guess. "If your father never spent much time at home, then he never spent much time with you, right, Naamah?"

She nodded her head and kept sobbing. I thought back to my own home, with a father who was often gone with the sheep. But at least my father loved his wife and loved his children and spent time with them as much as he could, working with them, singing songs with them, telling them stories of Father Adam. I bowed my head and said a silent prayer of thanks.

Naamah collected herself a little bit and kept talking in a nervous sort of way. "I was just a little girl. I didn't know what was going on. I just knew that something wasn't right. All I wanted to do was play with dolls, but Father didn't have time for dolls." As she grew into her teen years, and all of her brothers had moved out, Naamah was often caught in the crossfire of tension between Adah and Zillah. Naamah decided that she wanted to get out of the house as quickly as possible, to get married as quickly as possible to a man who would make her his first and only wife. She told her desire to her mother, who told her father.

Naamah was very surprised but pleased that her father approved of her idea. And he knew just the man, a brilliant scholar at the School of Humanism. Father had the man over for dinner, and I fell in love at first sight. His name was Mandrake, and he was tall, with long blonde hair like my father, with serious blue eyes that bore into my soul. "When Father unexpectedly offered my hand in marriage to him, Mandrake was startled. In the cutest way, he began to stammer and cough and state that he would have to talk with his father first. Of course, my father had already talked to Mandrake's father, and told the young man that he was certain that his father would approve. That evening was divine. Mandrake could not keep his eyes off of me."

As Naamah told her story, I could not help but think about romance in my life. I was only twelve, but I didn't look forward to spending the rest of my life as an old maid on Leper Island. Was God ever going to raise up a mate for me?

Naamah ignored my thoughts as she kept talk-ing about that night. "Everything seemed perfect. My father told Mandrake that he expected us to produce many beautiful, intelligent children who would advance the boundaries of human knowledge and culture."

"What did Mandrake say?"

Naamah giggled. "I giggled the same way when Mandrake, in his own serious way, told Father, 'I will do my best to produce such children.'" Then Naamah became more subdued. "Of course, none of us knew then how difficult and how long it would be before Mandrake and I produced children. It seems that I have always been doomed to disappoint my father."

She paused, and I asked how long it was before she married Mandrake. She smiled. "The only decision left was for Mandrake to gain approval from his father. He hurried home that night, talked to his father, then hurried back to my father's house to tell me that his father had approved. Within a month, on my eighteenth birthday, Mandrake and I were married."

Naamah happily told me that all of the family on both sides attended, even Adah. "Even Cain came to the wedding," she added.

"That's impressive," I blurted out, and I asked her why Cain accepted that invitation.

"Well," Naamah replied, "it certainly was unusual for Cain to attend something as lowly as a wedding, but he insisted. When my father told him of the marriage plans, Cain beamed and congratulated himself: 'It's not every day that the children of my two chief advisors are married.'"

A confused look spread over my face, but then the light of realization struck me like a gong. "You mean that Mandrake's father is Theron?"

Chapter Twenty-five

His Good Left Foot

I could not believe my ears. "You mean that Theron plotted to burn his five-year-old grandson at the stake, just because Javan had leprosy?" Such evil, violent wickedness staggered even my active imagination. I could not begin to understand how betrayed Mandrake and Naamah must have felt. I barely heard her words when Naamah further explained that Theron did not initially come up with the plan.

"Who did?" I demanded to know.

She tersely replied, "The child's other grandfather."

I became so jittery that I had to stand up and pace around for awhile on the sand. What twisted thinking process could possibly lead two grown men, at the height of reason and power, to plot such an unthinkable act? Try as hard as I might, nothing came to my mind. It didn't make any sense.

I walked back toward the hut, but Naamah had already walked outside. I looked at the tears coming down her face, stopped, shrugged, and had a quizzical look on my face. She walked over to me, and taking my hand, walked with me in the sand. "You see, Crista," she explained, "I had disappointed my father for my entire life. After so many years, when I finally produced a grandson, my father was so proud of me." Naamah then explained how Saaga lavished gifts on the baby boy and came up with extravagant plans for his life. Saaga would exult that Javan would be the next generation in the glorious human quest for progress and perfection.

My shoulders slumped. "And then at age five," I guessed, "Saaga discovered that his glorious golden grandson had leprosy."

"My father was furious," Naamah continued. "I was at his house when I told him, daughter to father. He ranted and raved that only defective parents could produce such a defective child. He demanded that Mandrake and I do something about our child. I demanded to know what he meant. His answer crushed me. He looked at me, his daughter, and demanded that I destroy my child."

Naamah stopped in the sand, and stopped crying. "I snapped. I looked at my father as I had never looked at him before. I planted my feet in front of him, looked up at his blue eyes, pointed my finger, and shrieked: 'You are a madman!'"

"Good for you," I said.

"I have never changed my opinion of my father nor regretted telling him what he really is. He swung his right arm and slapped me across my left cheek. I was stunned. But my feet remained planted. I stared into his enraged eyes, and with every ounce of power in my being, I warned him: 'Don't you dare touch my child.' Then I stormed out of his house, and I haven't been back."

*   *   *   *

Just then, we heard a familiar sarcastic voice: "Ladies, if there is ever a pause in your delightful conversation, would one of you mind getting me some water?" I walked over to the water jug, dipped out a cup of water, and returned it to the captain. After taking a few sips, the captain sounded almost cheery. "I have some good news," he said.

I just stared at him.

"Don't get so excited," he mocked. Then he said, "I moved my toes just a few minutes ago."

My eyes lit up. "Now, that is good news, Captain." I called out to Naamah, who rushed into the captain's hut. For the first time in days, the captain was civil, almost boyish. "Watch," he said, and then he wiggled the toes on his left leg. "Congratulations!" Naamah roared. "I must get word to Mandrake." Within a minute, Naamah was headed down the path to the village, leaving me alone with an awake patient.

"Mark my words, young lady," the captain exulted. "I'll be on my feet in no time. It won't be long before I get the two of us healthy people out of here."

"Healthy!?!" I laughed. "Do you consider yourself healthy?"

The captain smiled. "My current condition is obviously just a temporary setback. You know what I mean. You and I don't have leprosy, like all of the other hideous people on this God-forsaken island."

I corrected him. "Everyone doesn't have leprosy on this island. Look at Naamah."

The captain accepted my correction. "Yes, yes, Naamah is still clean, but she will never leave this island as long as Javan and Mandrake are alive. Family bonds can be most unreasonable at times."

I stared down at him. "You are despicable," I calmly stated, thinking of how he treated his own mother. "And another thing, Captain Blackheart, this island is not God-forsaken."

"Just a phrase," he said blithely.

"Captain," I said, uncertain of when to break the news to him, but feeling that today, when he had good news, that I could share good news with him, "I found God here on Leper Island."

"Oh," the captain mocked, "is your god a leper? Some people worship the sun, others worship the moon, or the stars, or a lion, or a tiger, or a frog. And now I learn that some people worship a leper."

I was not fazed by his insouciance. I calmly but quickly told him what happened just about sunrise on the day after we reached the beach. The captain was not impressed with my story. "It means nothing to me, but I'm glad if you have found some peace." Then he smiled. "Speaking of peace, would you mind getting me a piece of bread? That's the kind of piece I'm looking for."

After I served him a piece of bread, he commented that he had overheard a part of Naamah's story. I asked him if he had ever met Lamech-Cain. The captain said he had met the man a couple of times. "Twisted as a snake, he was," the captain explained, "and more slippery than an eel." I nodded my head in agreement and then exclaimed, "The heart of man is deceitful above all things, and desperately wicked." I was hoping that the captain would recognize his own sinful condition, but to no avail. "Young lady," he responded confidently, "I'm not sure what you think of this slave trader here in the hut with you, but you will have to admit that Lamech-Cain makes me look good."

I laughed out loud. "Yes, Captain, you sure look good today."

Amazingly, the captain laughed. "And I'm going to look gooder tomorrow, and gooder the next day, and before you know it, I'm going to get you and me out of here."

I stared down at him. "And just how do you plan on getting us out of here?"

"Simple," he said. "When I am on my feet, I will build us a little dinghy, with a sail and oars, and you and I will sail northwards, and in a week or two, we should hit the coast somewhere."

I kept staring down at him. "Are you out of your mind? I'm not going to get into a boat with you alone."

He blinked his eyes. "And why not? That's how we got here, and that's how we are going to get out."

"Captain," I explained, "it's not proper for a young lady to be riding alone with a man who is not her father or brother."

"Did your god teach you that in the last couple of weeks?" he smirked.

I glared down at him. "It's what my earthly father taught me at home, and what my Heavenly Father confirms in my heart."

"Now listen here, I will not break my promise. I told you that I would not leave you or forsake you. If I get a boat built, I'm taking you with me, and that's final."

I could tell it was useless to argue with him further, so I changed tactics. "When that day comes, we will see who forsakes whom. But until then, let's take one day at a time. Move your toes again, Captain."

He proudly moved his left toes again. "Great!" I said, really meaning it. "Now, move your right toes."

The captain stared at me. "Uhh, I can't . . ." and then defiantly, added the word ". . . yet."

I erupted in laughter. "Captain Blackheart, sir," I said, "do you want First Mate Crista to prepare the ship to set sail in the morning?"

He harumphed and asked, "Has anyone ever told you how irritating you are?"

Chapter Twenty-six

"Give me this water"

After examining the captain, Mandrake was very pleased with his improving condition. "You may walk again, Captain."

"Correction, Mandrake. I will walk again."

"That's the right spirit, too, Captain Blackheart, much better than the last time when you were trying to kill yourself."

"Temporary despondency, that's all," the captain said.

Mandrake then said that he planned to spend the next couple of days at the beach in order to further evaluate the captain's condition. I was certainly happy to give up my hut and sleep on the beach next to the fire.

After serving dinner to the captain, I made plans to clean up the area, refill the water jug, and other chores, just to get out of the way of husband and wife, but Mandrake had other plans. "Crista," he said, "I understand that you and Naamah had some interesting talks about our family backgrounds." When I mentioned that I was stupefied at how grandfathers could ever come to the point in their mind that they would plot the murder of their five-year-old grandson, Mandrake told me that he would like to take a little time to answer my questions.

As Mandrake, Naamah, and I moved away from the hut toward the fire, the captain interrupted.

"Mandrake, good fellow," he said, "may I have a word with you?" Mandrake went back to the captain's hut to check on his patient and was surprised at his request. It seems that the captain was not accustomed to constant company of women, and that the voices of Naamah and Crista were driving him crazy, and that he would appreciate hearing a male voice that night.

Mandrake chuckled, raised his left hand, and asked, "How close do you want me to get?"

"Well," the captain replied, "maybe you could sit in the doorway of the women's hut. I could probably hear you quite well there."

Mandrake was ever polite. "Do you know what I want to discuss with Crista?"

The captain replied that he would not mind hearing a little more about family history, especially since the captain had spent five years in Mandrake and Naamah's home during his childhood. So all of us got settled, and Mandrake started telling more about his family history.

Raised as the youngest son in the home of Chief Priest Theron, Mandrake was not expected to follow in his father's footsteps. Indeed, his father encouraged him to study any topic or topics which struck his fancy. Mandrake had the privilege of studying in many of the schools in the City of Cain, taking a great interest in animal husbandry and metal working. But his greatest love was philosophy, and his favorite field of study was Lamech-Cain's School of Humanism. Possessed of an apt mind and curious personality, Mandrake was fascinated by the possibilities of human fulfillment advocated by Lamech-Cain. Mandrake could still recite, nearly word for word, many

of the lessons which Lamech-Cain taught him and others
in their formative years. That night, in the door of the
hut, he recited some lessons learned fifty years ago:

> Man is the measure of all things. Our
> great City of Cain has led the world
> in cultural development because we
> humanists have freed man from the bonds of
> religious tyranny.

I couldn't help but pipe up. "But
Mandrake, Lamech-Cain was undermining Cain's own
cult of the Great Ebony Cow, wasn't he?"

"Good question, Crista. Cain was brilliant in his
own right, but he was not as sophisticated as Lamech-
Cain. Cain was only concerned with eradicating other
religions, such as the belief in the Redeemer as recorded
in the Words of God. Cain did not perceive that the
School of Humanism was advocating another religion
-- the worship of man."

> Without the restraints of religion, man is able to
> imagine, to explore, to create. We humanists have
> encouraged man to develop himself to his fullest
> capacity. The technological progress of our age
> is made possible only through the unshackled
> creativity of the mind of man.

Then Mandrake explained that he was not
opposed to technological progress, and that Lamech-
Cain, through his personal support of his sons' schools
of animal husbandry and metal working, had helped to

achieve great accomplishments which have benefited mankind. Where Lamech-Cain made his big mistake was ignoring God, ignoring that God was the God of creation and creativity, ignoring that Creator God gave us a mandate, as recorded in the Words of God, to "Be fruitful, and multiply, and replenish the earth, and subdue it."

> We must do our own thing. When you open your mind to all of the possibilities in the world, then you shall become as gods. Unshackle yourself from all forms of authority, including religion and your own parents. Then, and only then, you shall become your own god.

It sounded loony to me, but Mandrake explained that Lamech-Cain was attempting to elevate mankind to god status, not a new idea at all, but rather the same sinful mistake that Adam and Eve made in the Garden of Eden. "When they knew God, they glorified him not as God, neither were thankful; but became vain in their imaginations, and their foolish heart was darkened. Professing themselves to be wise, they became fools."

I pondered all of the sin that had fallen upon mankind because of man's desire to be as God. "So Lamech-Cain isn't as smart as he thinks, huh?" I asked.

"That's right, Crista," Mandrake replied. "The Words of God tell us that as the heavens are higher than the earth, so are God's ways higher than man's ways, and God's thoughts higher than man's thoughts." As I thought about how big my God was, I asked Mandrake what consequences that people such as Lamech-Cain would face someday.

He paused. "Understand, Crista, that I was headed down this same path. If God had not intervened and afflicted my son with leprosy, then the consequences in our lives would have been much worse."

The captain coughed, and spoke for the first time. "What consequences could be worse than leprosy, Mandrake?"

Mandrake was kind. "Captain, there are worse consequences that can happen to a man than concussions, knife wounds, and a broken back. When men change the truth of God into a lie, and worship and serve the creature more than the Creator, God will give them up to vile affections, even plotting to kill their own grandson."

The captain challenged Mandrake. "Surely not all men would ever become as low as Theron and Lamech-Cain."

Mandrake replied that different men fall into different sins. "As men do not like to retain God in their knowledge, God will give them over to a reprobate mind. Emptying themselves of God, men will fill themselves with all forms of unrighteousness, such as fornication . . ."

I piped up again. "Sounds like Letch."

Mandrake continued. ". . . wickedness, covetousness, maliciousness, full of envy, murder . . ."

I couldn't help myself. "That's what Lamech-Cain and Theron wanted to do."

". . . debate, deceit, malignity . . ."

I spoke up again, louder to make sure that Captain Blackheart would hear: "Like the spreading foulness of meat eating and slavery?"

"Exactly," Mandrake answered, continuing. ". . . whisperers, backbiters, haters of God, despiteful, proud . . ." Then he paused. "That's where I tripped up many times." Then he continued: " . . . boasters, inventors of evil things . . ."

I couldn't shut up. "Like Lamech-Cain having two wives?"

"Precisely." He continued. ". . . disobedient to parents, without understanding, covenant breakers, without natural affection, implacable, unmerciful . . ."

Naamah spoke up. "Javan's grandfathers developed into men who were without natural affection, implacable, unmerciful."

Mandrake finished his list of consequences. "Who knowing the judgment of God, that they which commit such things are worthy of death, not only do the same, but have pleasure in them that do them." He paused, then reminded us of Letch. "That wretched fornicator, without a doubt, was an evil man who obeyed not the truth. At the end, he found tribulation and anguish on Earth and the wrath of God for eternity."

It was silent for several moments. Then Mandrake asked a pointed question. "Captain, did you find yourself anywhere on that list?"

The captain was quick-witted. "You are implacable and unmerciful in trying to convert people to your new-found but old-fashioned religion. But to answer your question, maybe I'm on that list, maybe I'm not.

But surely you would agree that I am not as bad as Letch, or your father, or your father-in-law."

Mandrake was ready. "Maybe yes, maybe no. But God is no respecter of persons. As many as have sinned, whosoever has committed any of these sins, shall perish."

The captain paused. "I'll think about it." Then, he added, "Is there anyone here who could get me a cup of water?"

Mandrake asked me to hurry and get the captain a cup of water. As I poured the water down the captain's throat, Mandrake spoke up again. "Captain, whosoever drinketh of this water shall thirst again: but whosoever drinketh of the water that the Redeemer shall give him shall never thirst. Captain, my prayer for you is that one day, before your day of judgment, you will ask me or some other believer such as Naamah or Crista, 'Please, give me this water.'"

Chapter Twenty-seven

Rehabilitation

The captain's recovery was slow, painfully slow to all of us. He still had not gained the knack of being grateful for the humiliation of women changing his soiled linens.

But when he was able to wiggle his toes on his right foot about a month later, Mandrake decided that it was time for some rehabilitation. He instructed the captain to wiggle his toes every hour. "Even when I'm sleeping?" the captain joked.

Then Mandrake began to manipulate the captain's legs. He could lift each leg about six inches before the captain screamed in agony. Mandrake, in his serious way, told me to exercise the captain's legs just like that ten times every four hours.

"Are you crazy!?!" the captain screamed again. "That was agony!" Mandrake then explained to me, right in front of the captain, that the captain's muscles had weakened and become stiff all over his body. "If the captain ever hopes to walk again," Mandrake continued, "we must begin to rehabilitate those muscles, loosening them up and strengthening them." Then Mandrake told me to try it, and as an obedient nurse, I reached for the captain's left leg. The captain screamed. When I slid my left hand under the captain's left ankle and my right hand just above his left knee, the captain screamed. When I lifted his leg one inch, the captain screamed. When I lifted it two inches, the captain screamed. I contained an urge to lift his leg over his head. The captain was never a good patient.

*   *   *   *

Physical therapy seemed to never end. After working on his legs for about three weeks, I happened to see, when the captain didn't think I was looking, the captain lift his back slightly and move his right hand down his right leg to scratch his knee. I didn't say a word. I went over to the fire, where Naamah was baking some flat bread, and told her what I saw.

I told her a plan that was hatching in my brain. We sauntered over to the captain, and Naamah asked him how he was feeling. He told us that he was doing fine, which would have tipped off anyone that he was trying to hide something. I became very sympathetic to the inconveniences which a person in his condition had to suffer, such as not being able to feed yourself and not being able to get up to use the bathroom. The captain nodded each time until I said: "not being able to scratch your knee." His head froze, and his eyes turned away from us. Then I leaned over him, looked him in the eye, and said in my most syrupy voice, "Captain, if you ever have an itch, just tell me, and I'll scratch it for you."

The captain turned his eyes away and mumbled something like "Very kind of you, Crista." Then Naamah and I started to walk away, and I could hear the captain let out a deep sigh. When I stopped suddenly, I think the captain stopped breathing. I turned around and walked over to the right side of his cot, his eyes following me every step of the way. Then I raised my right hand in the air and declared: "Captain, something has come over me. I have a strong desire to . . . to . . ." And before I finished my sentence, I reached down and scratched his knee where he was scratching just a few minutes before.

The captain wiggled his body but could not escape the scratch. He glared at me and demanded to know, "Has anyone told you lately how irritating you can be?"

I looked down at him and replied, "Has anyone told you lately how stubborn you can be? How long," I asked, "have you been able to lift your back?"

"It's none of your business," he peeved.

I didn't waste a moment. I reached under his back and lifted him up about an inch. The captain screamed, and through gritted teeth, explained, "That's why I didn't tell you!"

*   *   *   *

Several more months went by, and the captain was finally able to sit up, which made our job much easier in several ways. Another month went by, and the captain made his first hesitant steps with the aid of two crutches which another leper had crafted. Mandrake assured the captain that the crutches had been boiled in water first. When the captain made his first unassisted trip to the private facilities, the rest of us cheered. When the captain returned, he even smiled and raised his thumbs up in victory.

A week later, the captain and I walked together to the stream as part of his physical therapy. There, I asked him to look into a pool of water that was not being stirred by the stream. When he looked into the water, he gasped. Then he looked at me and shouted, "You tricked me!"

I smiled. "What did you see in the water, Captain Blackheart?"

He looked again, then nodded his head: "I met someone I have never seen before -- a balding man with graying hair and graying beard." He shook his head. "I can't believe how much I have aged."

"It must have been the poison, sir," I said as kindly as possible. "But let me tell you, Captain, you look a whole lot better now than you did when we first arrived on the island."

He pondered that thought for a moment, then laughed. "We have come a long way, haven't we, Crista?" Stroking his graying beard, he playfully teased, "Maybe you should start calling me Captain Graybeard."

I chuckled. "I think Captain Blackheart still describes you better."

He laughed again. "Has anyone told you lately how irritating you can be?"

*　　*　　*　　*

The next day was my thirteenth birthday. Naamah went home to the village and baked a cake, and that evening, before the sun went down, the four of us had a little party. At times during the previous months, I hadn't known if I would ever reach my thirteenth birthday.

I had also reached a point in my life where my body was changing. Happily, Naamah presented me with two new dresses, and I gave her the biggest hug. I was so happy that I started to give Mandrake a hug, but he dodged my advance. Captain Blackheart, standing with the help of his crutches, scolded me, "Never do that again, Crista."

The party atmosphere was about to evaporate, but I was not ready to quit. I turned to the captain, told him that he was a humbug, and then gave him a quick hug, so startling him that he started to fall backward. As Mandrake moved quickly to catch the falling captain, Naamah laughed: "Don't do that again, either, Crista."

Three of us, at least, had a good laugh, and then even the captain laughed. Then he sighed, "It's been a long time since we could laugh."

*   *   *   *

The mood was less festive when Mandrake examined the captain the next morning after another round of physical therapy. "Captain, although you have made substantial progress, your right leg seems to be about two inches shorter than your left." Mandrake explained that the shortage was probably caused by a combination of the knife wound and broken back. When the captain asked how long it would take for his right leg to lengthen, Mandrake told him that it probably never would.

The captain's mood became somber. Mandrake told the captain how much of a blessing it was that the captain could walk at all, but that the captain would most likely walk with a pronounced limp, favoring the left side. "Any other good news this morning?" the captain sourly asked.

Mandrake told him that his back would probably give him occasional trouble for the rest of his life. The best way to avoid any further deterioration was for the captain to faithfully do his physical therapy every day and to walk every day, starting with short walks, then working up to three or four miles.

The captain walked several feet toward the beach, looked out on the horizon, turned back to us, and pronounced, "I'm going to keep walking, I'm going to get stronger, I'm going to build a boat, and I'm going to sail that boat away from here."

The rest of us clapped. But then, in his typical fashion, the captain spoiled the occasion. "And I'm not going to leave Crista here with a bunch of lepers."

Chapter Twenty-eight

Building a Boat

One morning several months later, when the captain was moving around quite well with just one crutch, Mandrake announced that it was time for Naamah to move back to the village, leaving Crista alone in the women's hut. When Mandrake finished making his announcement, the captain told us that he had an announcement to make, also. "I have come to accept that I will probably have this limp for the rest of my life," he said with a slight air of resignation. "In my journeys during the last thirty years, I have never met a captain with a pronounced limp," explaining that a captain must be strong and vigorous to lead men such as Letch with a stern hand.

"Therefore," continued the captain, "I have accepted, as my fate in life, that I shall no longer be a captain."

I bit my lip. I knew that was a tough decision for the captain, a decision which no one else could make for him.

Mandrake spoke up first. "What do you think you'll be doing with yourself once you get off the island?"

The captain nodded his head. "All I have ever known is the sea. I thought about just becoming a sailor, but I'm not sure that a captain would hire someone with such an obvious physical limitation. Besides," he added, "I know some sailors who would like a piece of my hide. No, the sailing life for me is over, I'm afraid, once I get off this island."

Naamah spoke up. "Good for you, Captain Blackheart. That means that you will give up slave trading?" she asked hopefully.

The captain scratched his beard, then responded. "Slave trading was lucrative as a captain, but I'm not sure it would be lucrative as a landlubber."

A thought entered my head, and as was typical, once it entered my head, it quickly exited my mouth. "Well, that's it then. I'm not calling you Captain Blackheart anymore."

The captain looked at me, considered my words, then nodded his head. "Well, I hadn't thought about that," he mumbled. Then he added, "Call me what-ever you wish." There was a brief discussion among the group, and then it was decided. We would call Captain Blackheart what Naamah called him when he was a child in her home: "Blackie."

*   *   *   *

The next morning, I was doing chores around our camp when the captain, I mean Blackie, called me to the door of his hut. When I peered inside, he was lying on his cot, looking up at the ceiling. "Is anything wrong, Blackie?"

"No, young lady," he answered. "I was just lying here when a couple of thoughts occurred to me."

"Like what?" I asked.

"Well," Blackheart confided, "first of all, I am going to teach you a trade."

I closed one eye and stared at him. "Like what?"

"Shipbuilding" he declared proudly. "You are going to help me build our boat."

I stared at him for a few more moments, then opened my mouth. "Are you out of your mind?"

"Young lady," Blackheart said soothingly, "don't you see? I can't have a bunch of lepers helping me build our boat. We are this close to going home," he argued, holding his right index finger just above his right thumb, "and now is not the time for us to consort with the lepers and become contaminated ourselves."

I shook my head. "Blackie, I don't know anything about building boats."

"I can teach you," he argued.

I wasn't done arguing. "Blackie, neither you nor I are strong enough to cut down trees and mill the planks."

"Crista, Crista," he said, as if lightly scolding a child who was not grasping a lesson. "I have already thought of that." Then he explained that he would design the boat, then ask Mandrake to organize men at the village to cut down trees and mill the planks and boards. "Of course, after all of the building supplies are delivered to the beach, you and I will treat each piece with that red cleansing fluid in order to kill any contamination."

I closed my eyes, recalling the stink and slime of that foul red liquid. Then I opened my eyes, stared at the captain, and politely told him, "You have got to be kidding!"

"No," Blackheart quickly replied, raising his eyebrows, "I am not kidding. Crista, this is the only way."

I lowered my head, raised my eyes skeptically, and told him that I would think about it.

"Pray about it, too," Blackheart added. "I am sure your god will agree with me that this is the only way to get you off Leper Island and back home to your family."

*   *   *   *

So I agreed to pray about it. As I started to walk away, Blackheart called out to me. "Crista, did you forget something?"

"What!?!" I replied testily.

"Crista, please don't get testy with me," he begged. "You haven't heard my other brilliant new idea."

I stopped, took a deep breath, and slowly turned around. "OK, Blackie. Five minutes," I said firmly. "You've got five minutes."

"That's all I ask, Crista." Looking above, he asked, "Is the ceiling flat?"

I stared at Blackheart for a moment, glanced unnecessarily at the peaked thatch ceiling, then stared again at him. Were we facing a new situation here, with mental problems replacing physical ones?

Blackheart set my mind at ease. "Of course I know the roof is peaked, not flat." Then he explained that he just had a brilliant idea: Build his boat with a peaked floor.

I nodded my head and stared at him some more. "Begging your pardon, Blackie, but seeing as how I have very limited sailing experience, perhaps you could explain to me what is brilliant about your idea?"

So he did. "You recall our dinghy, don't you?"

"How could I forget, Blackie?"

"Was the floor flat or peaked?"

"Flat, sir," I answered.

"Of course it was flat. All boats, all ships, have always been built with flat bottoms."

"Is that so, Blackie?"

"Yes, it is so, Crista." Then he began to explain how little dinghies and large ships such as the *Lucky Lady* have traditionally been built.

"It sounds like they were building a box, Blackie," I said to clarify shipbuilding in my mind.

"Precisely," the captain exclaimed, exhaling deeply. "I'm going to make a shipbuilder out of you yet."

For the next hour, Blackheart enthusiastically described his brilliant idea, and what the ramifications could be for the sailing industry. "Crista, one reason that captains prefer to stay close to the coast is that every ship is inherently unstable, both in its structural integrity and handling. Remember, ships are held together by tightened rope, and as time and pressure is applied, the ropes eventually weaken and snap." He demonstrated by putting the fingertips of his two hands together, then rapidly pulling them apart, making a snapping sound.

"As you recall," he continued, "I was nervous sailing away from the coastline on our ill-fated cruise." As I recalled my disappointment when the ship sailed west southwest away from the shoreline, Blackheart continued. "The only reason I risked taking the more direct west southwest route was that I was already behind schedule, and I wanted to hurry to unload my slaves on the markets down south."

Then he paused and looked at me in the eyes. "What would happen to the shipping industry if someone built a ship that had more structural integrity and better ease of handling? Why, of course, that person would make a killing, so to speak, as a shipbuilder. Very simply," he said, "we shall build a boat with a center beam, just like the center pole of the roof."

I looked up at the roof, then tried to envision flipping the roof over and resting it on its center pole. Every time, the roof fell over on its side. "Blackie," I said with some confusion in my voice, "I can imagine building a flat bottom boat on the ground, but every time I imagine building a peaked bottom boat, the boat falls over on its side."

Blackheart certainly had the design worked out in his head. "Crista," he replied, "we will build an elevated platform, sort of like a huge cot, upon which to build the boat." Then he described how he would place a huge beam on the ground under the platform, down the center, just like the center pole of the roof. Then he would attach the ship's ribs directly to the center beam. By adding siding and connecting the two sides with a variety of bracing, the ship would be more stable than any ever built before.

"Crista," he asked, "did you notice two things different about my boat design than all other previous boats?" As I thought about it for a few moments, I realized that his boat would not be held together by ropes. "Brilliant!" he shrieked. "No more . . . snap!"

As I was envisioning his boat, trying to figure out the second thing different, Blackheart interrupted me. "The second thing is a little more subtle, but equally fascinating -- the boat would have no bottom, only a center beam and siding."

I could envision that, but asked, "What difference does that make?"

Then he explained how the peaked bottom, so to speak, would sail or row faster than the traditional flat bottom boats and ships. "Imagine taking your hand, holding it up palm forward, and running your hand with its palm half submerged through a pool of water. Your palm will meet with a great deal of resistance as it shoves through the water." I was following him. "Then," he said, "imagine holding your hand with your palm downward, and then lowering your index finger, running your index finger through the water." As he described his actions, he then asked me: "Will the index finger meet more resistance, the same resistance, or less resistance than the palm of your hand as you shove it through the water?"

"Obviously, less resistance," I replied.

"Exactly!" Blackheart shouted in glee, thrusting his arms forward in a victory gesture. "Compared to a sluggish flat bottom boat, a peaked bottom boat will fly through the water, speeding its cargo to its destination, bringing great joy to the customers and great riches to the ship owner."

As I grasped what he was describing, I added a thought. "And the ship captain could take more trips every year, enriching himself even more."

Blackheart beamed at me. "Maybe I was destined to be injured and to spend so many months in recovery and rehabilitation. When we get off this island, we can make a killing!"

I laughed. "Blackie, if I ever get off this island, I'm going straight home to Momma and Daddy."

Chapter Twenty-nine

Sailing Away

Mandrake was very impressed by Blackheart's new ship design and promised to help him in every way possible. Mandrake even suggested how to solve one of the most ticklish problems -- how to get the boat into the water from the shipbuilding site further up the beach. As the shipbuilding platform was being built, Mandrake had one of the carpenters at the village make four wooden wheels. Whenever the boat was to be launched, the entire shipbuilding platform could be pushed down the beach into the surf.

Blackheart would only allow Naamah and me to actually help him build the boat since he did not want the boat contaminated by the touch of lepers. And before any beam or board or plank could be used, it had to be daubed in the foul red liquid in order to kill any contaminants. Of course, the red color faded over time, so Naamah and I named the little boat the *Pink Lady*. Blackheart was not amused.

It took many months for the boat to be built to Blackheart's specifications. It was not much larger than our dinghy, but it did have a sail attached to the mast which was anchored securely in the bottom of the peaked bottom boat. Blackheart had a hatch on the deck, with a place beneath for storage. Two small oars were latched on deck, and two larger oars were joined aft and could be reached by someone sitting in a short seat aft to steer the boat. Two long benches were built along each side, one bench for Blackheart and one bench for me.

When Blackheart showed me the two benches, I told him that I was not going to get on that boat with him alone. Either he would have to take someone else along with us or leave me behind. Blackheart was furious with me at first, reminding me that he had promised that he would not leave me or forsake me. "Fine," I replied. "Then bring someone else along with us." He gritted his teeth. "You know I can't do that." I smiled at him. "That's your choice, Blackie. Not mine. My choice is that I am not sailing away with you alone."

Blackheart and I settled upon a compromise. He would sail away alone. When he reached the coast, he would get another ship and come back for me. "And I won't delay," he insisted. "I will not leave you on this island."

*   *   *   *

Eventually, a date was set for Blackheart's departure -- my fourteenth birthday. We had a birthday party the night before, and early in the morning, a large group of men from the village, carrying several ropes, appeared for Blackheart's departure. Mandrake had earlier convinced Blackheart that Blackheart, Naamah and I would not be strong enough by ourselves to push or pull the shipbuilding platform into the water. "As long as none of us lepers actually touch your boat, but only handle the shipbuilding platform, I don't think your vessel will be contaminated."

Because I was much smaller than he was, Black-heart had asked me to stow his supplies aboard ship and man the vessel while the leper men used the ropes to slowly push and pull the platform into the water. I watched as the men waded deeper and deeper into the surf. When the boat finally floated free of the shipbuilding platform, Blackheart ordered me to toss out the anchor. After I did, I dived overboard and swam back to the beach, passing the men who were slowly pushing and pulling the platform back ashore.

Blackheart limped up to me as I came out of the surf. "It's not too late to change your mind," he pleaded. Unexpectedly, I hugged him, then backed away, and reminded him, "Don't forget your promise. Come back to get me as soon as you can."

He stood there, looking dejected, then slowly looked up. "Crista, I am a man of my word. I won't leave you or forsake you." Then he turned, limped into the surf, and swam to his dinghy. Then he climbed into the boat, weighed anchor, and set sail. He looked back and yelled across the waves, "I'll be back in two or three weeks. Look for me."

I stood there in the surf, waving goodbye, wondering if I would ever see him again, wondering if I would ever get off of Leper Island, wondering if I would ever return home. I stood there a long time, watching Blackheart sail away.

*   *   *   *

Mandrake agreed with my decision to stay alone in my hut, especially because Naamah was needed to help out at home with Javan, who had developed a bad cough. After one week, I packed up all of the things that I planned to take with me on my journey home.

I was surprised at how constantly and desperately I looked at the horizon. The closer the end of the second week came, I was almost useless around the hut, only performing the basic things to keep me going.

By the end of the third week, my doubts began. Was it possible that Blackheart, who utterly despised the lepers, was afraid to come back for me?

By the end of the fourth week, I was convinced that Blackheart had broken his promise. He had left me. He had forsaken me. I went to the village to seek some consolation from Naamah. Mandrake asked me to stay awhile, and I did so without question. Later that afternoon, he suggested that I return to the beach and continue my lookout. I had little hope left, but I followed his suggestion.

By the end of the sixth week, I knew what had to be done. I could not live the rest of my life alone on the beach. I decided that I would move near the village. My things were already packed up, so I determined to spend one more night in the hut, then make the short walk to the village in the morning.

The next morning, I cleaned up, ate some breakfast, gathered my things, and walked out of my hut. As I looked out at the empty sea one last time, I saw a speck on the horizon. As I watched in fascination, the speck slowly grew into a sail, and then into a ship.

I stood transfixed. I watched as the ship neared the island and weighed anchor. I watched as a balding, gray bearded man lowered the dinghy and rowed toward the shore. I watched as the man waved and shouted out my name. I watched as he reached the shore. I watched as he climbed out of the dinghy. I watched as he limped up the beach toward me. I watched as he lifted me up in his arms, hugged me, and cried with joy, "I'm back, Crista. I kept my promise. I didn't leave you or forsake you."

Then he put me down and took a step back. "I know you're upset, Crista," he babbled on. "It seemed to take forever to reach the coastline, and it seemed forever before I could find a ship. But I made it back, Crista. I'm going to take you home."

I took three steps back from him. A look of puzzlement came over his face. "Hey, look, Crista," he argued, "there are several sailors aboard that ship. You have no excuse not to come with me now."

I finally looked at him in the eye. His eyes were pleading, begging. I rolled up the left sleeve of my blouse. He followed my motion. When he saw the sore on my arm, he gagged and backed away, then turned and limped as fast as he could back to the dinghy. While I watched him, he climbed in the dinghy and started rowing back to the ship. Then, much to my surprise, he turned around and rowed back to shore. He stormed up the beach, furious, and when he reached me, he slapped me in the face. "You should have stayed away from those people!" he screamed.

I didn't even flinch. He fell to his knees and started crying. I backed away even further. He looked up at me, sobbing uncontrollably. When he finally calmed down enough to talk, he bitterly scolded himself: "Blackheart, you are no better than Lamech-Cain."

His eyes raised to mine, and for the first time in my life, Blackheart asked me to forgive him. He asked me to forgive him for slapping me and for taking so long to return. Then, he rose to his feet, took a deep breath, and, with a faltering voice, he said, "And please forgive me, Crista, that I am not able to take you home."

I was finally unable to hold back the tears. How desperately I wanted that man to hold me right then, to take me to the dinghy, and take me home. But now, I would never see home again.

Blackheart stood several feet away from me and asked me what I was going to do now. I told him that I was preparing to move to the village, to get on with the rest of my life, however long that might be. He asked me where I would live in the village, so I told him I would probably move in with Mandrake and Naamah.

Blackheart thought nothing of my comment. He asked if lepers ever married on Leper Island. I told him there was no prohibition against it. He asked if there were any suitable young men, such as Javan, whom I could marry when I became of age. "Javan was buried two weeks ago, Blackie," I informed him between tears.

Blackheart breathed deeply and shook his head. "You are not a lucky lady."

"I know," I replied without hesitation. "But my God won't leave me. My God won't forsake me."

Blackheart doubled over as if I had hit him hard in the stomach, wounded by my words more than I had ever hurt him before. When he finally looked up, he snarled and spat out the words, "Your god!?! What has your god done for you lately?"

I closed my eyes, having wondered the same thought so many times in the last two weeks. But I knew that my God was still watching over me. "Blackie, just go."

I was surprised that he hesitated. "I really don't want to go . . . alone."

I didn't say anything.

He stood there for over a minute, struggling inside. "Crista," he finally asked, "is there anything I can do for you?"

"Blackie," I responded, "there is one thing. Please don't tell anyone that I am here."

"Not even your family?" he pleaded.

"Especially not them," I answered. "I have been lost to them for nearly two years. As far as they know, I am dead. They do not need to know that their daughter is a leper."

Blackheart flinched at the word. He clasped his hands together, looked down at the sand for a few moments, and then, with an unexpected smile on his lips, looked me in the eyes and said: "I will go, Crista, but I won't forsake you."

Then he turned and returned to the ship. He waved, and I waved back, and I stood there a long time, watching Blackie sail away.

Chapter Thirty

Life Goes On

Naamah was still in mourning when I showed up late that morning. She insisted, though, that I unpack my things in their now spare bedroom. When I was finished, I came in and told her about Blackheart's visit. She sniffled and said, "You know, he was a good boy. I treated him like a son. I cried when he went back to live with his father at age ten, but that feeling is nothing like what I'm feeling now, Crista." As she started to sob again, I sat down next to her, folded my arms around her, told her how sorry I was, and stayed at her side for a long time.

At lunch time, I told Naamah to rest, that I would get the food ready. When Mandrake showed up for lunch, we three sat together and had our first meal as a newly formed family. Mandrake prayed for Blackheart's salvation, and for many other things.

After we finished eating, I asked Naamah and Mandrake what they thought of Blackheart's cryptic last statement. Naamah replied: "He was a good boy, Crista, and a man of his word. Maybe he will come back."

I was astonished. "To what!?!"

Mandrake softly answered: "To you."

*　　*　　*　　*

I became like a daughter to Mandrake and Naamah, and they became like parents to me. I helped Naamah around the house in the morning, and since I was healthier than most in the village, I did a variety of special chores around the village in the afternoon, such as bringing jugs of water to other houses and collecting fruit from the orchards and delivering it to any number of homes. My most important task probably was doing the wash for most of the village, especially the filthy rags which lepers, I discovered, accumulated at an astonishing rate.

One month after I moved in with them, Naamah instructed me in something I had never done before -- midwifery. Marriage was not prohibited on the island, and from time to time, a child was born. Since I was a cleaner leper than most, and since I was a female, Naamah asked me to help her when a leprous mother was in labor. I must admit that I took to it fairly well, joking with Naamah that Blackheart helped prepare me to be a midwife. When she asked how, I reminded Naamah of the blood and yuck in our dinghy while we were adrift at sea. And then, I said, "I'll never forget helping Mandrake treat Blackie's knife wound -- blood and pus and foul red liquid everywhere." And then I cried, realizing how much I missed Blackheart.

After Naamah cleaned up the newborn baby and while the mother rested, Naamah handed the baby to me. I marveled at the perfect nose, something not often seen on Leper Island. Then I asked Naamah if a leper should be handling a newborn baby, whose skin was so smooth and perfect. Naamah chuckled and said, "I'll recruit the next 'Clean' person I find."

We started talking about raising a child on Leper Island, and I mentioned that such a child would miss out on so many opportunities that the world had to offer. Naamah chuckled again. "Crista, I was raised in the cultural capital of the world. It's a shame that this child here will miss out on all of the things found in the City of Cain -- child sacrifice, slavery, prostitution, men having two wives, men beating their wives and children, grandfathers burning their grandchildren at the stake." Then she paused. "Frankly, Crista, I have never regretted raising my son Javan here on Leper Island. I have found more peace here on this little island than I ever found in the City of Cain."

I looked down at the little child, kissed his cute little nose, and decided to be grateful for whatever health and years that God would give me.

Naamah smiled and added a couple of more thoughts. "Crista, the first child I ever raised was the son of Captain Blackheart and his wife Lilith. Even though I have been marooned here on Leper Island, God saw fit to bring Blackie back into my life, and God allowed me to help him in his time of greatest need. That's not such a bad life, is it?"

I shook my head as she sniffled. "And Crista, I had always wanted a little girl, some little ball of spice to hug and kiss and play dolls with." She paused, then added, "But God never gave me one . . . until now." As I looked into her eyes, they were looking at me, brimming with tears. I placed the newborn on his mother's breast, then ran to Naamah. We hugged for a long time.

*   *   *   *

In the evenings, Mandrake often took me on field trips around the island. His scholarly enthusiasm rubbed off on me. "Nature is the best laboratory there is," he often said, "better than any metal working shop." He taught me how to make the green goop and even the foul red liquid. He taught me how to tell the age of trees and many other delightful wonders of God's creation.

One day, shortly after I moved to the village, Mandrake asked me if I would like to see the sheepcotes. I was delighted. As we walked there, he mentioned that he had helped to develop several different varieties of sheep. I looked at him quizzically. "My Daddy was a shepherd all his life. Sheep are sheep, aren't they?"

Just then, we came over a hill, and there before me were three different sheepcotes, with three different types of sheep. I was flabbergasted. One sheepcote had what I called normal sheep. Another sheepcote had black sheep. And still a third had white sheep with black ears and black feet and the thickest fleece I had ever seen. "This is marvelous!" I cried.

"I thought you would like it, Crista." Then he told me about techniques which he had learned from Jabal in the City of Cain about animal selection and reproduction. I was utterly fascinated. My Daddy, if he were alive, needed to hear about this stuff. "Why, Mandrake, we could make the world a much better place if more and more people followed these special animal selection techniques."

He nodded his head, then shook his head. "Yes, Crista, these techniques can be used for good . . . or for evil. Do you mind if I tell you a story?" I was all ears.

When he was a student, and later an instructor, at Saaga's School of Humanism, Mandrake had the privilege of helping Saaga develop certain scientific theories based upon Jabal's research into animal husbandry. Just as sheep or cattle could be improved from generation to generation by selective breeding practices, Saaga developed the theory that mankind could likewise be improved. Saaga saw himself as the pinnacle of human development and considered that it was his duty to advance the human race through selective breeding practices. His two oldest sons, Jabal and Jubal, proved to be such excellent physical and mental specimens that Saaga became convinced that he should produce more children.

I saw where this story was going, aghast that solid technical research was being corrupted for foul purposes. Saaga became enraged that his wife Adah could no longer bear children, leading him to the utterly corrupt idea and action of taking a second wife, Zillah. His explanation was always the same -- he was doing it for the good of the human race.

Saaga felt justified when Tubal-cain came along. What an exceptional aptitude for working with his hands that boy had! But then, along came Naamah, poor Naamah, who was beautiful to look at on the outside but who apparently had no special aptitudes beyond playing with dolls. Saaga was always disappointed with his daughter, looking at her as a bad experiment. "He married her off to me, hoping that through me, his daughter could develop exceptional children. To him, our marriage was first and foremost a scientific experiment."

"Crista," he said seriously, "scientific facts are true, but scientific theories may not be. When Naamah finally produced a child, Saaga was overjoyed. His theory could be tested in this new way. And praise the Lord, our son Javan was an exceptional child in many ways, truly a chip off of the old block. Saaga felt that his theory was validated.

Then, it was discovered that Javan had leprosy. The shock to Saaga was so great that I truly believe he lost his reason, if not his mind. Not only did he feel personally defiled in his blood line, but worse to him, his scientific theory was being undermined. His demand to Naamah to destroy her son was really a demand to terminate a bad experiment."

*   *   *   *

I felt unclean even listening to such a story. I was grateful that Mandrake walked us down to the sheepcotes, where I could pet the cuddly sheep. As I was admiring them, I asked Mandrake how far he thought that he could go in improving sheep through selective breeding practices. He said that was a question that Jabal, Saaga, and he had often discussed in the City of Cain.

Over time, Saaga developed variations of his earlier theory of animal improvement through selective breeding. Working with his son Jabal, Saaga tested out a theory that perhaps new kinds of animals could be developed through selective breeding. Saaga and Jabal tried to cross sheep with cattle, dogs with cats, and mice with chipmunks. As their various experiments failed,

Saaga asked the teachers and students at his School of Humanism for suggestions on how to achieve his desired goal of creating new kinds of animals.

"Mandrake," I asked, "did you ever come up with any such ideas?"

"No, Crista," Mandrake replied. "I never came up with any ideas how to create new kinds of animals, but I did offer to Saaga, in a written report, an explanation as to why it may not have been possible to create new kinds of animals. One week after I turned the report into Saaga, he stormed into my classroom, where I was preparing lessons for the following semester. 'I'm very disappointed in you, Mandrake,' he started."

"I take it that he did not like your report," I replied.

Saaga explained that Mandrake's report was not based upon science, but rather upon unscientific, untestable religious rantings. "I had theorized that new breeds of sheep could be produced through selective breeding techniques, but that perhaps new kinds of animals could never be produced because the laws of nature may contain uncrossable boundaries." Mandrake then explained how Saaga, in his highly intellectual style, criticized the "uncrossable boundaries" theory on two grounds.

First of all, Saaga flatly rejected the concept that there might be uncrossable boundaries in animal husbandry or any other field of human research. He insisted that mankind had made much technological progress because his School of Humanism had rejected the concept of boundaries of human knowledge and culture and that future technological and culture

improvements depended upon a consistent rejec-
tion of boundaries. "When I pointed out that his 'no
boundaries' approach was not a scientific principle but
rather a philosophical position, Saaga then launched
into his second criticism of my theory of uncrossable
boundaries."

Mandrake shook his head slowly as he started to
explain Saaga's second criticism. "If you recall, Crista,
I grew up in the home of Chief Priest Theron. Although
my father was a wicked man who taught and practiced
a false religion, he was nonetheless religious. Although
he and Cain rejected the truths of the Words of God, they
were familiar enough with the Words of God to twist
them, just as Satan did to Eve in the Garden of Eden."

I looked at the cute little lamb I was petting, then
asked Mandrake, "What do the Words of God have to do
with your theory of uncrossable boundaries?"

Mandrake explained that while growing up in the
home of the chief priest of the cult of the Great Ebony
Cow, Mandrake had been taught how to criticize the
so-called Words of God which were the foundation of
old-fashioned, obsolete, traditional religion. "Therefore,
I referenced in my report certain portions of the Words of
God, references which I can still recite today:"

> And God said, Let the earth bring forth grass, the
> herb yielding seed, and the fruit tree yielding fruit
> after his kind, whose seed is in itself, upon the
> earth: and it was so. And the earth brought forth
> grass, and herb yielding seed after his kind, and
> the tree yielding fruit, whose seed was in itself,
> after his kind: and God saw that it was good.

I was flabbergasted. "You wrote that in your scientific report!?!"

"Yes," Mandrake replied. "Saaga was furious that I would reference the so-called Words of God, or any religious writings, in my scientific report, declaring such sources as unscientific. When I replied that I did not espouse the truth of those Words of God, but only referenced them as one possible explanation as to why Jabal's experiments failed to produce new kinds of animals, Saaga snickered and pointed out that the religious writings talked about grass, herbs, and fruit trees, not animals."

Mandrake sighed, then continued. "I was not yet ready to give up my theory. I pointed out to Saaga that the only reason that I referenced that religious source was because it provided an explanation for the obvious truth that plants 'yield seed' and that plants reproduce only 'after his kind.' Well, Saaga ignored what I had just said and instead declared that my report should have talked about animals, not plants. That's when our argument went downhill."

"Downhill!?!" I blurted out.

"Yes," Mandrake laughed. "I kindly pointed out that my report did talk about animals, not just plants. When I took the report and started pointing out subsequent passages discussing animals reproducing 'after his kind,' Saaga admitted that he had not read that far in the report. Then, he grabbed the report from me, threw it down on the ground, and stomped on it. He looked me right in the eye and declared, 'If a scientific theory is based upon concepts found in religious writings, then the scientific theory is not science at all, but rather religious rantings, and therefore cannot be true science.'"

"Saaga was beginning to get a little upset, huh?" I said.

"At that point, I still was not ready to give up on my theory. I kindly pointed out that, regardless what any particular religious writing may or may not say, it was true that animals reproduced 'after their kind.' At that point, Saaga pointed his finger at me and said, 'If I had known that you held these beliefs, I never would have let you marry my daughter or hired you as a teacher at the School of Humanism.' I wasn't a believer then, and this conversation occurred several years before Javan was born. I did not want to lose my teaching position, so I made it clear to Saaga that I did not believe these religious writings, that I only referenced them. He pondered that explanation for several moments, then announced to me a new policy that went into effect immediately: 'Scientific research and reports shall be based upon science, and not upon religious writings, which will hereby be banned from all further research and reports.' I told Saaga that I could live with that policy. Then he turned to walk out of the classroom. When he reached the door, he turned and snidely remarked: 'The only kind of animal reproduction I want you to be concerned about is between you and my daughter Naamah.'"

*   *   *   *

The thought of his son Javan, recently buried, brought a tear to Mandrake's eye, and then I started tearing up also. He walked over to one of the sheep and absently scratched its ears. "God created life in that first week of creation, Crista, according to God's rules and God's boundaries. We may not understand it all, but life goes on."

Chapter Thirty-one

Surprise Visitor

I celebrated my fifteenth birthday in the common room at Mandrake's house. He and his wife presented me with gifts, we ate a cake, and despite missing Javan dearly, we focused that day on the blessings of God on our life. Then there was a knock on the door. All of us wondered who the visitor would be. I secretly hoped that one of the villagers was at the door, ready to hand me another gift. Mandrake got up from his chair, walked to the door, and opened it.

All of us gasped. It was Blackie. "Hello, Mandrake," he said. Adjusting his eyes to the dim light in the common room, he greeted Naamah, then me. Then, much to everyone's surprise, he gently stated, "I have a birthday gift for Crista." He told us that the gift was down at the beach, and that Mandrake and Naamah could also come to see it.

This was all so shocking and mysterious. Mandrake turned to us and said, "Ladies?" Both Naamah and I leaped out of our seats and followed Blackheart and Mandrake. Blackheart did not say anything further until he limped quickly out of the village. He was obviously relieved. He slowed down to allow me to catch up to him. "Crista," he smiled, "I have kept my promise."

*   *   *   *

Waiting on the beach was a brand new dinghy.
"I have named her *Crista*." Then pointing at *Crista*, he
presented the little dinghy to me as a birthday gift.

I was flabbergasted, speechless. Blackheart
leaned over to Mandrake and quipped, "She looks rather
fetching with her mouth shut."

I finally opened my mouth. "What do you want
me to do with her, Blackie? Escape the island?"

Blackie laughed. "No, no. Just use the *Crista*
for recreational purposes around the island, to help you
remember the old days when you were First Mate Crista."

I started to cry, my mind flooding with memories of the *Lucky Lady*, the dinghy, the rock. Without
thinking, I rushed over and hugged Blackheart, who at
first did not resist. Then he slowly stepped back and
said, "Is it proper for a young lady to hug an older man?"
I was not deterred. I leaped upward and kissed him on
the cheek. He was so surprised that he fell backward on
his bottom.

"Let me show you something else, Crista." Just
then, a sailing vessel came sailing around the trees. We
all watched it fly across the water. I screamed: "A
peaked bottom ship!?!"

Blackie beamed. "You are witnessing the maiden
voyage of the *Indomitable*, the first peaked bottom ship."
As we all watched the ship with fascination, Blackheart
told us his interesting story.

Captain Blackheart was the most notorious
slave trader in the known world, but because of his
pronounced limp and changed appearance, with his
balding head and gray beard, no one recognized him when
he finally reached the coastline. One of the first things

he inquired about at the first inn that he came to was whatever became of the *Lucky Lady*. A couple of sailors told him that the *Lucky Lady* had disappeared over a year ago. No one ever saw Captain Blackheart, his crew, or the slaves again. Some people had said that they saw smoke far out into the sea one day, so some people thought that maybe the galley caught fire and burned up the ship. But nobody knew for sure. Some people said that the *Lucky Lady* was a cursed ship because both the elder and younger Captains Blackheart had been such cruel slave traders. If no one had seen hide nor hair of the people on that ship in over a year, then they surely became shark food.

Blackheart decided that day that Captain Blackheart should remain dead. From that first day ashore, whenever anyone asked him his name, he told them that his name was Graybeard.

After his first unsuccessful visit back to Leper Island, Blackheart decided that he would pursue a career as a shipbuilder, incorporating his new design into current models. He first started making peaked bottom dinghies, and after those became successful, he built his first ship, the *Indomitable*, now on its maiden cruise.

*   *   *   *

Naamah asked Blackheart if his shipyard was in Livernium. He explained that since it would be more likely that people would recognize him in his hometown, he located his new business in another port, the City of Shorr. Then he asked me if we could take a private walk on the beach.

"Crista," he asked, "have you ever heard of the City of Shorr?" I told him I thought that Momma had mentioned once or twice to Daddy that she would like to take a vacation there, but that life intervened, and Momma had never made it.

"I hope it was not too presumptuous of me, Crista," he said, "but while in the City of Shorr, I made inquiries about your father."

I was stunned. I couldn't believe this. "What!?!" I screamed. Mandrake ran over to find out what was wrong, but I waved him away. "Is he alive?" I naturally asked first.

I was so relieved when Blackheart smiled. As he told the story, I was amazed at God's amazing grace. "Apparently, the blow by Arphaxad's club transformed your father's life. According to my sources, your father went on some sort of journey in search of God, your God, Crista." I was so excited, my knees started to shake. "Apparently," Blackheart continued, "your God lives in more than one place, because, according to my sources, Enoch found your God."

"Praise the Lord!" I shouted. I ran back to Mandrake and Naamah and shared the glorious news. "How marvelous are His works," Mandrake said, lifting his hands to the sky.

I insisted that Blackie tell all three of us the rest of the story. "I only have a few details, but probably the most peculiar concerns Arphaxad."

I gasped. "Oh no! Don't tell me that Daddy had another encounter with that thug!?!"

So Blackheart explained that Arphaxad had been developing his own slave trade. I interrupted him. "So that's the source of your information, huh? Don't tell me you are getting back into slave trading, Blackie."

He acted offended. "I would never dream of it. Those people know me too well. But," he added, "I do know where the slave traders hang out, and I do know how to listen." He then told us how Daddy had defeated Arphaxad at the City of Gom.

"Yea!" I yelled. "Did he kill him?" I asked expectantly.

"No, Crista, that's where the story gets peculiar." Then he described how Enoch took Arphaxad to his homestead to recover from his wounds.

Naamah smirked: "I'm sure Sarah was thrilled with that development. Sometimes husbands do the strangest things."

"Now, I'm offended," Mandrake laughed.

"Please, please, Blackie, tell us more of the story." So he told us that apparently, through some obviously special circumstances, the thug Arphaxad became a believer.

My jaw had never dropped so low in all my life. I could not believe my ears. "Arphaxad!?!"

"I don't believe in miracles, Crista. I don't even believe in your God. But the proof is in the pudding. Enoch and Arphaxad are now traveling together, telling people about their experiences."

*   *   *   *

All of us stood there, hardly able to believe such a story. Then, Blackheart became more serious.

"Mandrake," he said gently, "I am sorry to inform you that your father has apparently passed away."

Mandrake's eyes became very large, then he dropped to his knees. Naamah instantly knelt down by his side and put her arm around him. After a few minutes, he looked up at Blackheart and asked him how it happened. Blackheart explained briefly that Cain sent Theron out with a squad of priestly guards to assassinate Enoch and Arphaxad as the two preachers made their way to tell the people of the City of Cain about their religious experiences. No one knows what happened, but Enoch and Arphaxad arrived unharmed in the City of Cain. Neither Theron nor any of the guards was ever heard from again.

Mandrake rose from his knees, hugged his wife, and sighed: "The judgment of God is certain." As the rest of us paused to allow Mandrake time to reflect, Mandrake began to talk. "It is remarkable how the story of Enoch has so many parallels to the story of Captain Blackheart," he said, startling all of us. "The blow to the head, the new career, the unexplained disappearance of people trying to kill you. God truly works in mysterious ways."

Naamah interjected. "Blackie, you said that Enoch and Arphaxad arrived in the City of Cain. Did my father or Cain stop them from preaching?"

Blackheart smiled again. "The last thing I heard about those two was that they preached about their God from atop the Tower of Cain, and then made a safe escape from the city."

"Unbelievable!" Naamah declared. "I wish I could have seen that."

Chapter Thirty-two

Escape from
Leper Island

Every year for over two hundred years, Blackie came to my birthday party. He always had a dress for me and Naamah, supplies for the village, news of my family, and of course, a view of his latest peaked bottom ship on its maiden voyage. He was a man of his word. He never broke his promise.

It was through Blackheart that I kept up with family news, especially after 720 A.C., when Blackheart also brought us the news that an old crusty slave trader named Peleg had been led to the Lord by Enoch that year. Blackheart said he had been careful to avoid meeting Peleg personally since they had known each other for years in the slave trading business. Although Blackheart looked completely different with his balding head and gray beard than when he was captaining with a full head of black hair and short, trimmed black beard, Peleg would have known who he was the moment he looked into Blackheart's eyes.

But Peleg and his crew kept the seaport full of news of Peleg's favorite prophet. One day, the City of Shorr buzzed with news that the Prophet Enoch had destroyed a temple in the City of Gom after Cain and Zaava sacrificed a baby girl on the temple altar. Blackheart wept with me when he told me that the baby's mother was my old friend Adah. Then, in his own way, Blackheart rejoiced with me when he told me that Adah had found my God.

*   *   *   *

As the years rolled by, Blackheart shared more family news. I was astonished to hear that Arphaxad and Adah were married, and then a little later, even my brother Methuselah married a woman named Martha. I was glad for all of them, glad that God had allowed my brother to marry and to have children. I was not bitter, but from time to time, despite my best efforts, I occasionally asked God why.

*   *   *   *

My relationship with Blackheart changed as my teen years flew by. It was obvious that he was developing an affection for me, but it was an affection which could never be fulfilled. Nonetheless, he came back every year. He said more than once that he received more than we did from his gifts to us -- he received an oasis of peace in a cutthroat world.

Of course, his attitude toward lepers, at least one leper, changed over the decades. The sores spread over my body, and year by year, I became more and more hideous. It was funny, but each year, Blackie said I was more and more beautiful. He was lying, of course, just trying to lift my spirits on my birthday, but it did help that he visited every year.

*   *   *   *

As the years and decades and centuries rolled by, many changes took place at Leper Island. Every three or four years, new lepers would be dropped off by their family members, and we would find room for them in the village. Mandrake conducted hundreds of funerals, and eventually, I attended his funeral. I had the privilege of speaking at his funeral, the last funeral I ever spoke at. I said simply, through my badly diseased throat, that "Mandrake led me to the Lord and has left a legacy that will forever endure."

In the year 937 A.C., Naamah passed away. I wasn't able to speak at her funeral service. By then, I was pretty much reduced to mumbling indistinct syllables. But by some special act of grace, I was still able to whistle. When I whistled "They That Wait Upon the Lord" at Naamah's funeral service, many people began to cry.

*   *   *   *

That year, I was the only one on the beach when Blackheart arrived for my annual birthday party. I knew that something was wrong when Blackheart did not lower the dinghy of his new peaked bottom ship. Instead of placing my annual gift and other supplies into the dinghy, he dove overboard and swam to shore.

There arose a distressed look in his eye when he limped toward me. He blurted out, "Crista, this is my last voyage to Leper Island," then he collapsed to his knees and began to weep. He looked like a man who needed comfort, but I was not in any condition to comfort a "Clean" man. I had sores all over my body, and much of my nose was gone. Yet, he had not hesitated to rush to me. The only comfort I could give was prayer. "Dear God," I prayed, silently moving my jaw, "help this man."

Blackheart looked up and actually whispered, "Thanks." Then he hurriedly explained that over the years, many competitors had copied his peaked bottom design. Many of them were building ships that did not meet his quality specifications, using cheaper lumber, cheaper nails, cheaper sails. By cutting their prices, they were cutting his throat. Finally, before he lost the business altogether, he sold the business. "This is the last ship I will ever build, Crista, the last maiden voyage."

I wept. These annual birthday parties were the one thing that kept me going all year long. What was I going to do now? Was the Lord telling me that my time on Earth was drawing to a close?

Blackheart rose to his feet and actually grabbed my shoulders. I was so shocked that he grabbed me, then shocked again that he did not let go. "Crista," he said with every ounce of determination in his body, "I will not leave you. I will not forsake you."

I forced myself to spring away from his grip. I pointed to my ravaged body, then in the direction of the village. All I could say were two words: "Uh-kee! Uh-kee!"

Blackheart lunged toward me again and grabbed my shoulders again. "No, Crista," he explained, "I'm not staying here with you. I'm taking you with me."

I looked out at the ship anchored off the beach, and I saw several sailors on the deck handling some sort of strange contraption. I slipped from Blackheart's grasp and started to run back toward the village, crying as I went, "Uh-kee! Uh-kee!"

"Crista," Blackheart cried out, "you must stop!" He pleaded, "I need your help!"

I slowed down, then stopped in the sand. I have always been a sucker when someone needed help. I did not know how I could help Blackheart, but at least I could listen. So I turned to him and motioned to explain himself. I was not prepared for his explanation. Father Adam was dying of leprosy, and there was no one to take care of him.

I closed my eyes. How ironic, I thought, that Adam, who had brought sin into the world, was dying of leprosy, one of the best illustrations of the destructive power of sin. But I did not yet understand how I could help Blackheart, so I looked at him and shrugged.

"Crista," he replied, "let me take you off Leper Island and transport you to Father Adam's homestead so you can take care of him in his dying days."

His words did not make sense to me. Soon, in a year or two or three, someone was going to have to take care of me. Why should Blackheart go to all this trouble to take me to Father Adam's homestead when Adam might be dead before we arrived? I shrugged.

Blackheart looked like his favorite puppy had just died. "Crista," he said very simply, "I made a promise long ago that I will not leave you, that I will not forsake you." Then he limped toward me, saying as he went: "I'm not staying here, so I'm taking you with me."

Tears welled up in my eyes, but I raised my right hand, which still had its thumb and all four fingers, and motioned to Blackheart to stop. I nodded my head, turned around, and motioned for him to follow me.

*   *   *   *

Within an hour, Blackheart was rowing me and my few earthly belongings in the dinghy *Crista* toward the waiting ship. Blackheart had draped an oversized hooded cloak over me, and personally helped me into the ship and into what appeared to be a large cage on the deck. Once I was securely inside the cage, he rowed the *Crista* back to shore, then swam back to the ship. We set sail immediately.

It was a strange sensation, after over two hundred years, to sail the sea again with Captain Blackheart. We seemed to be flying, much faster than when we sailed the *Lucky Lady*.

Blackheart kept me away from the crew, and the crew certainly drew a wide berth around the strange cage with the hooded lady. Blackheart waited on me hand and foot, saying it was an honor to do so. "You took care of me, hand and foot, for nearly two years when we were both much younger. It is a little thing to take care of you on this journey."

It was almost like a dream. I loved the sensation of flying through the water. I marveled when the seagulls appeared in the sky. I marveled when I saw the coastline. I marveled when we docked so smoothly at the City of Shorr.

Blackheart escorted me personally off the ship, then had his sailors offload the cage and place it in the back of a waiting wagon, along with some other supplies. When Blackheart helped me up into the wagon, I thought he was going to return me to the cage, but he surprised me. He patted the other end of the front seat and motioned for me to sit down.

We left immediately on the road north. I wanted to stay and sightsee in the town, but I knew that would be impossible. As we reached the outskirts of the city, Blackheart looked over at me and smiled. "Well, Crista, after all these years, it looks like you and I are on the road again."

* * * *

On our sixth day of travel, I noticed that the pine trees were thinning out and the cedar trees were becoming more dominant. On the seventh day, the road looked familiar. We were on the road to Gom! My heart started beating very quickly, and I longed to catch a glimpse of the old homestead. Blackheart read my heart and asked me if I wanted to ride by to see the old place. I thought about it for a few seconds, then shook my head. My family must never know.

Later that day, we drove through the City of Gom. It had changed little since I last saw it. The south gate looked the same, the marketplace was still busy, and the fountain still flowed. There was not any evidence that a temple had once been built in the marketplace.

When we drove by Ludim's blacksmith shop, I saw him walking from his shop toward the house. It was a strange sensation seeing the first familiar face I had seen in over two hundred years. He looked very thin, very gray, very old. Then I giggled as I thought to myself, He's aged better than I have. Blackheart looked down at me, then followed my gaze to the old man walking up his front porch. "Someone you know, Crista?" I smiled and nodded.

* * * *

The journey to the City of Cain seemed to take forever. Everything in that city was very bright and fresh and new, flourishing under the leadership of Cain, with able assistance of his chief advisor, Lamech-Cain. But as we drove through the marketplace, with men and women selling their own bodies as well as selling slaves, I realized that the city was a whited sepulcher, filled with dead men's bones.

After two more days of travel, Blackheart pulled the wagon atop a high hill. He pointed toward the north-west, and I spotted a very bright hill in the distance. "That's a sand dune, Crista. The wilderness is moving quickly toward Adam's homestead, but it has not arrived yet." He rattled the reins, and the horse plodded on over several more hills, until we came to a small hill overlooking a very old, very decrepit homestead.

* * * *

I stared at Adam's homestead, my new home, my final home, as Blackheart drove the wagon down the hill and parked it in front of the house. Blackheart unharnessed his horse, returned to the front seat, then helped me stand up. He surprised me when he hugged me . . . and held on tight . . . like he never wanted to let me go.

He looked down at me, and with tears in his eyes, he spoke his last words to me: "Well, Crista, this is the end of the trail." Then, he surprised me again. He leaned over and kissed me on top of my head. As I looked up at him in surprise, he escorted me into the cage. He hopped off the wagon, hopped on the horse, and rode off.

He stopped at the top of the hill. He waved, and I waved, and then Blackie rode on. I knew that I would never see him again.

Epilogue

The common room in Enoch's homestead was quiet, and the sun had retired for the night long ago, when Crista finally finished her story.

"That's one of the most beautiful stories I have ever heard," Adah said.

"I am so proud of you, Crista," Sarah added.

Methuselah leaped from his seat. "Hey, Mom, do you have any more cookies?" Then he wandered into the courtyard.

Elihu asked, "What do you think you are going to do now, Crista?"

Crista sighed. "I don't know. Right now, I'm just glad to be home."

Elihu pressed forward. "Do you think you will ever see Blackheart again?"

Crista sighed again. "I don't know. I haven't seen him for the last three years."

Methuselah walked back into the common room, chomping on a cookie. "Most everybody in the City of Shorr knows who Graybeard the Shipbuilder is," he said between chomps. "But after he sold his shipbuilding business three years ago, word went out that Graybeard went back to sea as a common sailor."

Adah asked more pointedly, "Do you want to see him again, Crista?"

Crista closed her eyes and sighed deeply. "I don't know. Blackie is part of my old life, and I have a new life now. Besides," she shrugged, "he's a sailor, not a believer. There could be no future for the two of us."

Elihu nodded.

Acknowledgements

Crista's Story, Book 4 of *The Methuselah Chronicles*, is dedicated to Joy and Casey King, my fantastic daughter and favorite son-in-law, who live in the big city of Little Suamico, Wisconsin. Joy, the General Editor of all Glory to Glory projects, and Casey, our Graphics Designer, are the faithful laborers who take my manuscripts, place them in the proper book format, and then deal with all of the administrative headaches of getting the book printed. Please allow me to also acknowledge Joy as the inspiration for Crista's spunky personality.

The Foreword to this book was written by my pastor, Pastor John Jones, of Lighthouse Baptist Church, Ashtabula, OH. Pastor Jones, my favorite creationist scholar, continues to be a big supporter of all of my writing projects. I can truly say that without Pastor Jones, there would be no Glory to Glory Ministries.

The covers of the first three books in this series were graphically produced by Casey King. For the cover of Book 4, we used an artist for the first time, Nancy Colle, art teacher at Heritage Christian School, Cleveland, Ohio.

Just as with the earlier books in the series, the book editor of *Crista's Story* was Mary Storm, who puts her heart and blood (i.e., lots of red ink) all over my manuscript.

Special thanks also go to my wife Jan and to my son Daniel and his wife Jessica, all of whom read early drafts and provided helpful comments. Special thanks also go to Daniel and Jessica for giving Jan and I our first grandbaby, Grace Kathryn Hamilton, born on July 1, 2004.

Coming soon . . .

Book Five of
The Methuselah Chronicles

[T]he [R]oad
to [N]oah

by Terry Lee Hamilton

Crista's touching reunion with her mother Sarah is spoiled by a murderous assault on Enoch's homestead by the thug Og. Taking up his father's mantle and the staff of God, Methuselah travels with his sister to the enemy's stronghold in the City of Cain for an explosive confrontation with Saaga, Cain's successor as leader of that wicked city.

After a truce is declared, Methuselah and Crista develop a revival ministry which confronts the increasing ungodliness and violence in the world before the Flood. But the forces of evil continue to plot to thwart God's promises of the birth of Noah and the coming of the Redeemer.

Crista's long wait for the return of the love of her life is finally realized, just in time for her and Methuselah to race home to face Og and to prevent the fiery destruction of the first family of faith.

If you liked the characters, action, suspense, and romance of *Methuselah's Father*, *The First Prophet*, *Bound for Glory*, and *Crista's Story*, you will love *The Road to Noah*. Order each book in *The Methuselah Chronicles* by:

°°   writing Glory to Glory Ministries, 1813 East 45th Street, Ashtabula, OH 44004.

°°   e-mailing terry@glorytogloryministries.com.

°°   going to the web at glorytogloryministries.com or amazon.com.

God bless you!